"I can't be in a relationship with you."

Kelly felt like someone had dropped her from a great height. She couldn't speak. Couldn't think. She'd experienced something similar during Danny's breakup speech. Except…this felt worse.

Her feelings for Alec were a different story. She'd hardly been able to believe that someone as wonderful as Alec wanted to kiss *her*. As it turned out, he *didn't* want to.

Alec was looking at her with something like concern. "I hope we can still be friends," he said.

She forced herself to nod.

"Do you…do you want to stay home today? I'd love to have you come shopping."

Kelly *didn't* want to come. She wanted to go inside and hide out with Pokey. But she'd promised Zinnia she would come.

"Sure," she said, putting on her first-grade-teacher enthusiasm. "I want to go."

"You're sure you're okay? I'm really sorry, Kelly."

"It's fine! You're right, it's much better to be friends."

If she said it often enough, maybe she'd start to believe it herself.

Lee Tobin McClain is the *New York Times* bestselling author of emotional small-town romances featuring flawed characters who find healing through friendship, faith and family. Lee grew up in Ohio and now lives in Western Pennsylvania, where she enjoys hiking with her goofy goldendoodle, visiting writer friends and admiring her daughter's mastery of the latest TikTok dances. Learn more about her books at www.leetobinmcclain.com.

Books by Lee Tobin McClain

Love Inspired

K-9 Companions

Her Easter Prayer
The Veteran's Holiday Home
A Friend to Trust
A Companion for Christmas

Rescue Haven

The Secret Christmas Child
Child on His Doorstep
Finding a Christmas Home

Redemption Ranch

The Soldier's Redemption
The Twins' Family Christmas
The Nanny's Secret Baby

Visit the Author Profile page at LoveInspired.com for more titles.

A Companion for Christmas

Lee Tobin McClain

LOVE INSPIRED
INSPIRATIONAL ROMANCE

LOVE INSPIRED®
INSPIRATIONAL ROMANCE

Recycling programs
for this product may
not exist in your area.

ISBN-13: 978-1-335-59836-3

A Companion for Christmas

Copyright © 2023 by Lee Tobin McClain

For questions and comments about the quality of this book, please contact us
at CustomerService@Harlequin.com.

Love Inspired
22 Adelaide St. West, 41st Floor
Toronto, Ontario M5H 4E3, Canada
www.LoveInspired.com

Printed in U.S.A.

For now we see through a glass, darkly; but then face to face: now I know in part, but then shall I know even as also I am known.

—*1 Corinthians* 13:12

To reader and friend Mary Kay Biddle,
who came up with the name Pokey.
Perfect for a retired racing greyhound!

Chapter One

Kelly Walsh carried her last box of supplies into the big river house and then kicked the door shut behind her, blocking out the December cold. She stomped the snow off her boots and shook it from her hat, then set the box on the wood block table and rubbed her cold hands together. "We'll unload the boxes and then turn on the fireplace," she assured her dog, Pokey.

The greyhound was shivering despite her red fleece jacket. She looked up at Kelly with trusting brown eyes.

"Okay, okay. We'll do the fireplace first." Kelly patted the dog's head and then led the way to the living room, checked the thermostat for the furnace, and turned it up. She knelt on the chilly wooden floor and studied the gas fireplace, then switched it on. Immediately, warmth radiated outward. Pokey leaned against her, wagging her tail.

"Who's a good dog?" Kelly put an arm around Pokey. Trained to give comfort to schoolkids and nursing home residents, the therapy dog wasn't a personal service dog. She and Kelly worked as a team to help others. Still, the sensitive greyhound often gave comfort to Kelly as well. No doubt Pokey had sensed her anxiety about their temporary new home.

Through the tall front windows, the sky glowed deep pink, edged with gold and purple. Kelly had intended to move in well before dark, but her first graders had been wild today, and she'd spent extra time cleaning up her classroom and adjusting her lesson plans to account for the kids' pre-holiday excitement.

"Lie down, I'll be right back." She pointed to the braided rug in front of the fire and then trotted up the stairs. Time for flannels and a hoodie and some fuzzy slippers. Being all the way out here in the woods, away from her usual small-town neighbors, she could dress for total comfort and not worry about anyone dropping by.

The air upstairs was colder, so as soon as she'd changed, Kelly hurried back downstairs. She checked on Pokey, who was snoring delicately. Good. Kelly would unpack her kitchen boxes first.

Putting away supplies for her Christmas baking project—flour and sugar and spices—

comforted her. She'd made the right choice, housesitting for the rest of December in a place with a huge kitchen. The extra money she made from her baking side hustle would help to get her overly generous parents out of their financial hole.

Also, planning for the homey activity of baking soothed worries she'd barely acknowledged in herself. She'd do fine here. After all, it wasn't like she was in Antarctica. She was still in Pennsylvania, very near the small town where she'd grown up. Her parents lived just two miles away, as did most of her friends.

Until today, she'd lived in the garage apartment at her parents' house. Which had been fine when she'd been a happily engaged woman planning a Christmas wedding. It made sense to save on rent.

Once the engagement had ended earlier this fall, she'd started to think that a twenty-nine-year-old woman basically living with her parents seemed a little pathetic. Not to mention the fact that her parents needed to rent out the apartment to a paying tenant. She knew it, even if they denied it. And they'd stubbornly refused to let her pay them rent.

It wasn't even her first broken engagement, but her second. The first engagement had been short-lived, lasting only a couple of months just after college, but this second one had been serious. She'd thought it was the real thing.

The troubling part was that when the relationship ended, she hadn't even been crushed. Embarrassed, yes, but also relieved.

Which showed how much she knew. She'd gotten over Danny so quickly. How could she have thought a marriage between them would work?

Given her history, no way was she up for a third try. Hence, she'd embarked on a plan to become independent, a happy single. First up was house-sitting, then, as soon as she could swing it financially, a little place of her own.

A car door slammed outside.

Kelly jumped and pressed a hand to her pounding heart. She wasn't expecting company. She backed into the living room and knelt beside Pokey, who'd lifted her head and was looking toward the back door.

"You could at least stand up!" she whispered to the dog. Greyhounds weren't known for their guarding abilities.

She heard another car door, then a deep male voice.

Her heart pounded harder, and she grabbed her phone. Should she call 911 or her dad?

Pokey gave a little bark and advanced toward the back door.

Even gentle Pokey was braver than she was. She needed to get a grip. It was probably a lost pizza delivery guy.

If that was the case, then she'd look like a fool and word would spark through the small-town gossip wire. *Kelly Walsh got scared housesitting and called the cops.*

It would be another reason for her parents to tell her to come back home, for her friends to advise against living alone. She needed to be strong, independent, and brave. She grabbed the decorative fireplace iron and advanced to the doorway into the kitchen.

A key sounded in the door, and then it opened, and a large, jacketed man burst in, half turned to the side as if he was hiding something behind him. He shook snow out of his hair, his eyes scanning the room, and he spotted her in the doorway instantly.

Was he hiding a gun? She raised the fire iron. "I'm calling the—"

"Get out. No squatters—"

Recognition dawned. They both went silent and stared at each other. Beside her, Pokey whined.

She let her makeshift weapon clatter to the floor. "What are you doing here?" she burst out, beating him to the question. Seriously, Alec Wilkins, her older sister's high school boy-

friend, had just shown up, unexpected and un-
invited, in her temporary home?

He was still a handsome guy, worth notic-
ing if you were interested in dating and relationships.

But she wasn't. *And you could never get him,*
her critical inner voice said. *You couldn't even
keep Danny as a fiancé.*

"Kelly?" His face broke into a slightly confused smile. "I guess you're not some squatter,
but what are you doing here?"

Kelly opened her mouth and then closed it,
too full of her own questions to answer his.

"Daddy?" came a small voice.

Alec shifted, and she saw he was holding a
young child, had been concealing her behind
him. The little girl was blond, whereas Alec
had dark hair, but they shared the same gray-
blue eyes.

Alec had a child?

"This is Daddy's old friend, Miss Kelly,"
he said, stroking the child's hair. "This is my
daughter, Zinnia," he said to Kelly.

The little girl, who appeared to be about
three, looked at Kelly briefly and then snuggled closer into Alec's chest. "Cold," she said.

At which point Kelly realized she was leaving
a man and child freezing at her doorstep, not to
mention the fact that the open door behind them

was letting in icy air. "Come in, let's get you both warm. I have a fire going." She gestured toward the living room and then sidled around Alec to shut the door behind the pair. Up close, she saw the day-old stubble on his cheeks and the tired circles beneath his eyes.

She led the way into the living room and looked back. Alec was toeing off his own shoes, and then he knelt and unzipped Zinnia's coat and pulled off her little pink boots. He carried the child into the living room and headed for the fire.

He set her down, kneeling and keeping an arm around her.

Kelly's dog came closer, obviously drawn to both the strangers and the warm fire.

"Hi, doggy," Zinnia said, reaching toward Pokey.

Alec pulled her hand back and frowned.

"Pokey's gentle," Kelly assured him. "She's actually a therapy dog, so she's used to kids."

"You're sure?"

"I wouldn't take her to preschools if I wasn't."

"Okay. Pet her on the neck, like this, sweetie." Alec reached out and gently scratched Pokey's neck and chest.

Zinnia sank to her knees and rubbed Pokey's neck, and soon the big dog lay down, panting a smile.

Alec looked up at Kelly. "So, you first. Why are you here?"

"I'm housesitting for the month of December," she explained. "The Baldwins are doing an extended Christmas thing in Bali."

He frowned. "John gave me a key a couple of years ago. Said I could stay here when I was in town. I've done it several times before."

"Oh, right. I guess I'd heard that. You didn't check with them before coming?"

"I didn't. Usually I do, but they're hard to reach. And...things got a little busy."

"Where's Zinnia's mom?" Kelly asked. Then, realizing the question sounded blunt, she waved a hand. "Sorry. Not my business."

While they were talking, Zinnia had come over and leaned against her father's leg. "Mommy went to heaven," she said now, and then stuck her thumb in her mouth.

Oh, no. Kelly wanted to reach down and scoop the little girl up into her arms. "I'm sorry," she said, looking at Alec with concern.

He nodded. "She's been gone six months." He was studying the child. "Zinnia doesn't always remember."

"I 'member." Zinnia's forehead wrinkled. "I 'member Mommy."

Kelly's heart ached for the little girl, but there was nothing she could say, no way to fix the situation. To judge from Alec's expression, he felt the same helplessness.

Had he been married to Zinnia's mom? Regardless, he had to be grieving her loss.

Wind whistled around the old house, and tapping sounded against the windows, like stones being thrown. "I wonder if that's sleet," Kelly said, looking in that direction.

"Probably. I heard while driving in that there's to be a wintry mix tonight."

"Yeah. My favorite."

Zinnia yawned and lay down by the fire, her head on Pokey.

"Is that okay?" Alec asked. "The pup won't mind?"

Kelly nodded. "Pokey's the most easygoing dog around. That's why she's such a great therapy dog." Kelly could tell she was about to go babbling on and on and forced herself to stop. She needed to focus on this situation of them both wanting to stay in the same house and figure out what to do.

It was difficult, though, when his piercing blue eyes seemed to look into her soul. Or maybe he was just staring at her outfit, because…rats. She was wearing the ugliest clothes in the state of Pennsylvania. She looked down at her hoodie. Was that…yes. Daffy Duck. Her cheeks heated.

"We'd better figure out what to do," he said, frowning as he pulled out his phone. "I'll see if I can find a hotel for the night."

The wind was still howling. Could she send a tired-looking man and a young child out into this weather?

"It's a huge house. I guess… Do you want to stay tonight and figure it all out tomorrow?"

The question hung in the air as Alec followed Kelly into the kitchen. Kelly Walsh. Warm, friendly and wholesome. The girl who'd befriended the outcast kids and collected canned goods for hungry families and sung in the church choir.

The exact opposite of her sister. And the last person in the world he wanted to see, let alone stay with.

Did he want to stay tonight? Well, yeah, on one level, he did. It was warm and cozy inside, cold and snowy outside, and Zinnia was exhausted.

When he'd dreamed of home while serving his country in the Middle East, he'd dreamed of a place like this. When he'd learned he was a father and that his ex-girlfriend was sliding into drug dependency, he'd imagined getting full custody of his daughter and raising her in a home like this.

The horrible thing that had happened six months ago, and the challenges of learning to be a full-time single dad, had pushed all fantasies about a Norman Rockwell household out of his mind. Suddenly, tonight, they were coming back.

But would three-year-old Zinnia notice the slight resemblance between Kelly and her mother? Would Kelly realize that Zinnia looked like Chelsea?

And even if that didn't happen, could he live with himself if he didn't tell Kelly the truth?

He'd changed so much since the single night of drunken romance that had resulted in Zinnia's conception. He'd been on leave, and Chelsea had been lonely, and they'd hooked up for a brief reprise of their high school relationship.

After that, his life had taken a different turn. He'd stopped drinking and partying and he'd become a Christian. Chelsea had gone in a totally different direction.

He was too tired to stop the racing thoughts in his head. He gripped the doorjamb to make sure he stayed upright.

"I think you'd better sit down." Kelly pulled out a kitchen chair and waved him toward it.

He glanced back into the living room. Zinnia still lay with her head on Pokey, eyes closed, breathing regularly. The dog seemed to be sleeping, too.

He took the chair Kelly had indicated, and she put a cup of fragrant hot chocolate in front of him. "Sorry it's from a pod," she said. "I'm just moving in, so I don't have the supplies for homemade."

He took a sip of hot chocolate. "Thank you. This is fantastic."

She sat down across from him with a mug of her own steaming beverage. "How long have you been driving? From where?"

"Phoenix." He stretched his tight shoulders and rolled his neck from side to side. "We did stop at an army buddy's place in Missouri, so it wasn't straight through." Alec's friend and his wife had graciously offered to take care of Zinnia for a few hours so he could sleep and she could play with their toddler and toys and dog. But she'd been needy, out of sorts with all the changes in her life. As dusk fell, her crying had awakened him, and he'd realized he just needed to push through to Holiday Point, driving through the night when she was more likely to sleep.

"Still, we're a long way from Missouri. You need to stay tonight. When did you last eat?"

He frowned, thinking back over the blurry hours of driving. "We got fast food at lunchtime today. Again, not ideal, but…"

"Fast food French fries can cure a lot of problems," she said, and smiled. Instantly, she went from cute to beautiful.

Yes, her mouth was too wide and her figure too curvy for a modeling career like Chelsea's. Her hair was pulled back in a casual ponytail, with unruly strands escaping around her face. She lacked her sister's high cheekbones, classic model slenderness and perfect hair.

Yet he couldn't take his eyes off her. Couldn't control the way his mouth went dry and his heart rate hiked up. Could barely keep himself from leaning closer. "Thanks for not judging," he said finally, to break the silence.

"I have some homemade mac and cheese, courtesy of my mom." She walked over to a cooler and pulled out a big glass container. "Want me to heat some up? Does Zinnia have any allergies?"

He shook his head. "No, but I think she's out for the night. And you don't have to make food for me. We have some stuff in the car."

She was already scooping mac and cheese onto a plate. "There's way too much here for me to eat myself. I don't know if you remember my mom, but to her, food is love."

And that apple didn't fall far from the tree, he thought, watching Kelly bustle around the kitchen. She was obviously at home there, and she seemed glad to interrupt her evening to prepare food for unexpected guests. Soon, there was a steaming plate in front of him.

"How are your folks doing?" he asked between bites.

"They're okay. Dad's working for the county now. Mom got laid off." She held up a hand as if to stop him from asking the next logical question. "I don't know if you heard…" She paused and drew a deep breath. "Chelsea passed away in June."

His heart thumped extra hard. "I did hear. I'm sorry for your loss."

"I'm mostly sorry for Mom and Dad. This has been incredibly hard on them. Chelsea cut off contact. We hadn't heard from her for years, until we learned she'd died."

"That must be hard." Guilt washed over him. Could he have talked Chelsea into reestablishing those family ties?

"It *is* hard. I hate what she did to them, and to other people in this town."

That was what Chelsea had meant when she'd told him not to reveal that she was Zinnia's mom. She hadn't wanted Zinnia to be tarred with the same brush she had been.

"You're planning on staying in Holiday Point?" she asked, taking his empty dish to the sink.

"I hope so. If I can find work and a place to stay. It's a good place to raise a child."

"It is," she said. "Just…don't play up the fact that you dated Chelsea once and you'll be fine. Some people are still bitter toward her."

"Right. Sure." Her words pushed him out of the relaxed state he'd started to get into, what with the warm house and the food and her friendliness.

He had to be careful. He couldn't let the secret out.

He didn't want to cause pain to the Walshes, who'd always been kind to him. And he didn't want to break his promise to Chelsea.

Most of all, he didn't want Chelsea's reputation to taint her daughter. Zinnia deserved a fresh start, and he would try his best to give it to her.

Which meant keeping his distance from Chelsea's family and especially her sweet sister. Starting tomorrow.

Chapter Two

The next morning, the world was sparkling.

With ice.

Kelly had to windmill her arms just to keep herself from falling when she let Pokey out to do her business.

She studied the sky. Partly cloudy. So it was anyone's guess whether sunshine and the plows could clear the roads, or whether more snow would strand them here.

Please, not stranded. She and Pokey had a gig in town, helping out with a Santa event.

Plus, it was a little odd to be here with Alec and Zinnia.

But in any case, they'd all be here together this morning. She was already planning to bake the last of her cookies for delivery today. As long as she was in the kitchen…

She turned on some Christmas music low and

started mixing up pancake batter. She kept it as quiet as possible. Alec and Zinnia had to be exhausted.

She had so many thoughts about Alec. She remembered him from high school days because he'd been kind of notorious. A strong athlete who quit the football team senior year without explanation. A guy who all the girls loved, but who never went to dances.

Of course that kind of puzzle had been of massive interest to Chelsea. She'd gone after him, dated him hot and heavy for a few months. And then he'd left for the military. Chelsea had continued to get into more and more trouble, and eventually, she'd left for parts unknown.

The pancake batter finished, Kelly pulled out the cookie dough she'd made last night and started scooping out spoonfuls onto her biggest cookie sheets. She'd never understood why her sister had gone out of control. She'd had the same good childhood that Kelly had. When she'd started getting into trouble, their parents tried everything: church, counseling, punishment and tough love, forgiveness. None of it had worked.

Chelsea had gotten into drugs, and eventually, she was thought to have gotten a couple of other kids hooked. She'd borrowed a car and wrecked it. A family who didn't know her reputation had hired her to babysit, and she'd stolen money from them and left the kids alone. Somehow, she'd escaped jail time for any of her crimes and misdemeanors, but her reputation in the town was still awful.

Her parents had tried to get her into counseling and rehab, but none of it had stuck. Eventually, she'd thumbed her nose at her family and left town.

Kelly missed the sister she'd been close with as a little kid. She'd cried plenty of tears when she learned of Chelsea's death.

But she was angry, too, at the way Chelsea had hurt their parents. Had hurt all of them, really.

She slid her cookie trays into the oven. Hearing a few noises from upstairs, Kelly pulled her thoughts away from her sister and focused on cutting up fruit to go with the pancakes, humming along with the music.

Soon there was a sound from the doorway and little Zinnia came into the room, rubbing her eyes. She walked right over to Kelly. "Mommy," she said, lifting her arms.

Kelly's heart turned over as she lifted the little girl into her arms.

That was the problem with her plan to avoid another engagement that might fail. She'd always wanted kids.

She felt the weight of the sturdy toddler in her arms, smelled the sweet fragrance of her scalp. She turned off the stove and carried her over to the table and sat down, rocking her back and forth.

"I'm sorry she bothered you." Alec came into the room, sleepy-eyed and stubble-faced, buttoning a flannel shirt over his T-shirt.

"Daddy!" Zinnia struggled out of Kelly's arms and hastened to her father, who picked her up and gave her a quick, distracted kiss on the head before settling her in his arms.

Alec was as beautiful as a work of art, especially holding his daughter in such a loving way, and he was in her kitchen. Well, the kitchen they were fighting over, she supposed. That, or sharing. She cleared her throat. "There's about an inch of ice coating everything outside," she said. "You may as well sit down. I'm making pancakes."

Zinnia clapped her hands. "Cakes!"

"You don't have to cook for us, I hope you know that. But…pancakes? We love 'em."

"Good. Get whatever you both want to drink. There's coffee and orange juice and milk." She turned on the gas stove beneath the cast-iron griddle she'd found in the cupboard.

Moments later they were gathered around the table with steaming, fragrant plates of pancakes in front of them. She was surprised to see Alec lower his head for what must have been a quick prayer, and she hastily did the same herself. The circumstances were so strange that she'd nearly forgotten.

After he'd cut up a pancake for Zinnia and they'd all taken a few bites, he put his fork down. "Thank you again for the breakfast and for letting us stay last night."

"Of course. The mix-up wasn't your fault, and with this weather, I'm glad you're not out on the road." The timer dinged and she hurried to pull her cookies out of the oven.

He served Zinnia some fruit. "I'm surprised you're housesitting during the holidays. Thought you'd want to be with your family."

"Well…" She returned to the table and took a sip of coffee. "I love my family, but I needed to get out of town for a bit."

He lifted an eyebrow. "Things too hot to handle? Did you rob a bank?"

She laughed. "Nothing so exciting. No, I… The truth is, I was supposed to be getting married over the holidays." For a moment, visions of the poinsettias and holly she'd planned on, the deep red trim on the dress she'd bought, and the Christmas cookie cutter favors she'd planned for the guests, all flashed before her eyes.

"I'm guessing the wedding is off. I hope it was a mutual decision."

She sighed. "Not exactly. He ended it. Right after we sent out the invitations."

"Ouch. I'm sorry. That stinks."

She nodded. "Thanks. In retrospect, I think he was right. We cared for each other, but maybe not the way a married couple should." Even as she said it, her stomach twisted. When Danny had told her he didn't feel as strongly as he should, she'd read between the lines: he wasn't attracted enough. It had done a number on her self-esteem, already a bit battered by having grown up with a sister as gorgeous as Chelsea.

"Better to find it out before the wedding than after, I guess. But I'm sure it's rough."

She nodded. When she'd realized that she, too, hadn't felt as strongly as she should, her eyes had been opened. She was bad—really bad—at choosing men. "The hardest thing is how nice everyone's being. Treating me like I'm made of glass. The whole town knows both of us—he's the youth pastor at that megachurch out on 221—so it was all pretty public. I needed to get away." She went to the counter and tested her cookies, then started moving them onto a cooling rack.

"Makes sense you wanted to escape. This is a great town, but it's also gossip central."

"Yeah." It made her think about his reputation growing up. His family hadn't been stable, and there had been times when his father or uncle got in trouble with the law. Nothing major, as she remembered, but "drunk and disorderly" was grist enough for the rumor mill.

Her family had always been on the positive side of the gossip chain, until Chelsea had gone off the rails. Then they'd all learned what it felt like to have other people stop talking and look away when you came into a room or a shop.

"You can see why I wanted to get out of town. But I still need to be close to my parents, so this place is perfect." She gestured around them. "I hate to make you and Zinnia find another place to stay, but I have plans for this big kitchen." She explained about her cookie side hustle. "Is there any place else you could stay?"

He blew out a breath. "We can't stay with my parents. It's not a good environment, out there." He waved vaguely toward the hills where his family lived. "That's why this place seemed like a good solution, but I'm sure there's some other way."

"You definitely want to stay in town for a while? Rather than going back out west?"

He nodded. "We're staying here."

"Can I ask why?"

He spread his hands. "It feels like home, a

good place to raise a child. Plus, my grandma lives here, in the senior apartments. She's disabled, but she'll help however she can. And my brother Cam and his wife are over in Hunter's Grove."

"Could you stay with them?"

He shook his head. "They're bursting at the seams. They live in a one-bedroom place with two kids and another on the way. Saving up for a bigger house."

"Hmmm." It looked like the solution to their problem wasn't for Alec to leave. "I need to stay here to do my cookie baking project," she said, waving a hand toward the dozens of cookies now cooling on the large counter. She started pulling out boxes to pack them in. "Exhibit A," she said. "There's just not room at my parents' house."

"Could we stay here together?"

She bit her lip. "That's what I'm trying to figure out. I mean, the house is huge. Plenty of space, three bathrooms…there's only one kitchen, but aside from that, you could host an army here."

"Will it damage your reputation?"

What a quaint way of putting it. "I mean… people who understand the situation will be fine with it."

"Your folks are pretty traditional."

"True."

"They didn't like me when I was dating your sister."

"That's true, too." Kelly started lining boxes with tissue paper. "But you were the least of the problems in Chelsea's life." She shrugged. "Look, part of what I'm doing here is trying to get over worrying about what other people think. If people are going to judge us for sharing a giant house so you and your child can have a place to stay and I can bake cookies to help my parents…" She lifted her hands, palms up, her conviction growing as she spoke. "That's their problem. I'm not going to let it bother me. Does it bother you?"

He barked out a laugh. "Believe me, my reputation in this town is already shaky, because of my family. Staying here with an upstanding member of the community, like you, won't do *me* any damage."

"I hope you're right." She started tying up her cookie boxes with red and gold ribbons.

He stood and began clearing the table, waving away her protests. "If I'm staying here, I'm doing my share."

Zinnia reached for him, and he swooped her up and set her on the ground. "Go get your frog," he said.

She toddled away and soon returned with not

only a frog, but a whole armful of stuffed animals. She set them down in a row.

"Do you want to feed your animals breakfast?" Kelly asked. She handed the child a small bowl and spoon. "I think that's applesauce in there."

Zinnia studied the empty bowl and then nodded. "It is," she said. She started spooning the pretend applesauce into the mouths of her animals.

Kelly checked the time. "Okay, I need to take off."

"You're good driving on these roads?"

"No choice," she said. "We have a therapy visit to a Santa event this morning, and then I'm going to deliver cookies to a few families. Six," she added, checking her list.

"I can drive you. I have new snow tires."

She waved a hand. "No need for us to do everything together," she said. "Come on, Pokey." She put the dog's Christmas sweater on her and started loading cookies into the car, walking carefully on the ice. Alec followed her out with the rest of the boxes; when she turned around, there he was, and she caught a whiff of a soapy, spicy, masculine scent.

She backed up quickly. As soon as he'd set the cookies down on the passenger seat and she'd gotten Pokey inside, she nearly dived into the driver's seat and started the car.

He was saying something, but she was too disconcerted by her own strange reaction to open the window and listen. "I'm late," she said, tapping her wrist where a watch would be. Then she backed out of the driveway and started down the road.

Thirty seconds later, her car slid.

She pumped her brakes. No effect.

Her car glided gently into a snowdrift.

Her cookies flew to the floor. Pokey yelped.

The hit was gentle enough that she barely felt it. She turned around to Pokey and petted the shivering greyhound, examining her for any sign of injury. Her tail wagged. She was fine.

She was bending to check on her cookies when she heard a shout. A moment later, Alec was tapping on her window, Zinnia in his arms.

She lowered it. "I'm fine, but...is that ride still available?"

Every lamppost along Holiday Point's Main Street was decked out with an evergreen wreath, bright red bow and white lights, with snow providing a twinkling garnish. Clusters of bright-coated people strolled along shoveled walkways, looking into colorful shop windows. In the distance, down at the point for which the town was named, Alec could see a huge Christmas tree.

"Did they decorate like this when we were younger?" he asked Kelly.

"Not as much, I don't think. People are working hard to make sure the downtown survives."

"So we're calling it a downtown now?" He pulled the car into a diagonal parking place.

"Well, sort of." She flashed him a grin. "I'm sure it's nothing like what Phoenix had to offer."

He thought about that. There'd been plenty of museums and architecture and live music, but also the kind of dangerous people and places that had led to Chelsea's downfall. *Don't go there,* he told himself. "What Phoenix definitely didn't have," he said, "was a white Christmas."

Zinnia started bouncing around in her car seat. "Santa! Santa!"

Sure enough, the jolly old man was climbing out the passenger side of a rusty pickup truck just ahead of them. He headed toward the shops as the truck drove off, and Alec frowned, recognizing his gait. "That's my brother Fiscus."

Kelly was trying to manage Pokey's leash and her boxes of cookies. She looked up and tilted her head to one side. "Is it?" Then she cut her eyes to Zinnia and back to Alec. "No, that's Santa," she said.

Of course, he'd better watch what he was saying or Zinnia would lose her belief in Santa almost before she'd realized who he was.

"San-ta! San-ta!" Zinnia struggled with the car seat's buckle.

He wasn't sure he wanted to confront Fiscus just yet, but he couldn't just drop Kelly off and drive away without disappointing Zinnia. She wanted to see Santa.

Oh, well. This was as good a chance as any to get a feel for how the town was now. He wanted to make sure his tentative plan to relocate here with Zinnia was the right one.

"Just leave the cookies in the truck," he said. "We'll stay and help you make your rounds after the Santa visit."

"Oh man, that would be great, but are you sure? Tell you what, if you and Zinnia want to leave, one of my friends will be able to drive me around."

Of course they would, because if it was anything like their high school years, Kelly had a ton of friends. She'd gotten along with everyone: the popular jocks, the troublemakers, the drama and music crowd, the nerds. Chelsea had spoken of her sister's many friends in a disparaging way that Alec had known, even then, was a cover for envy.

Chelsea had been so breathtakingly beautiful that she hadn't lacked for people who wanted to hang around her, especially boys. But her so-called friends had been burned by Chelsea's mean side. Few had stuck around, including him.

They approached the tall old building that had once been a clothing store. Shabby and empty throughout Alec's childhood, now its white bricks had been freshly painted and the windows were decorated with old-fashioned Christmas displays: a toymaker in his shop, raising and lowering a hammer; pajama-clad children decorating a tree; the wise men gathering around the manger.

Inside, the place had apparently been converted into a vendor's market, with everything from antiques to handicrafts to dolls. People crowded the aisles, talking and laughing. Christmas music played, and the fragrance of hot chocolate and cider filled the air.

Zinnia gave a little hop beside him, and when he saw her wide smile, Alec's heart melted. He hadn't seen a whole lot of that smile since they'd started their journey east. Even before that, she'd become a serious kid since Chelsea had died. He wanted her to be happy and carefree.

Like the two little boys who nearly careened into them.

"Whoa, Micah, Josh, slow down." Kelly knelt and hugged both boys. "This is Zinnia, who's… visiting town for a while."

"Cool." But the boys were too wound up to

stay in one place, and they ran off down the aisle toward the area where Santa was apparently to visit.

His brother. Man. Alec just hoped Fiscus was sober enough to act the part of Santa.

"Kelly! Pokey! Over here!" A woman in an elf costume was beckoning.

"I have to get set up for the kids who are scared of Santa. Don't leave without letting me grab my cookies, okay?" She smiled and headed toward the elf.

Alec followed more slowly, holding Zinnia by the hand. She looked around, curious and excited, taking it all in but a little hesitant.

A blond woman in a tight-fitting, neon-green sweater put a hand on Kelly's shoulder. "This must be such a hard time for you," she said.

"Thanks. I'm fine." Kelly kept moving.

The woman followed. "How awful that Danny dumped you like that! I mean, the invitations were out, and I'm sure you'd already paid for the hall and everything. That must have been such an expense!"

Was that concern on the woman's face, or glee? Alec saw Kelly's shoulders slumping. Instinctively, he hurried to catch up. "Maybe we'll stick close for a few minutes, since Zinnia is so fond of Pokey," he said, falling in step beside her.

Sweater woman veered off, eyebrows raised. She hurried over to another woman and started talking, quietly and rapidly.

"Everything okay?" he asked Kelly.

"Remember what I told you about why I don't want to be in town?"

"Everyone feels sorry for you?"

She nodded. "I guess it helps to be here with a good-looking man," she said and then flushed.

She thought he was good looking? Nice. "Happy to serve as your escort, if it helps."

Before she could answer, Santa, aka his brother, came out from the back of the vendor area with a wave and a "ho-ho-ho." He climbed into the throne-like chair set up for him between two vendor stalls crowded with antique-looking toys. A whoop went up from the kids, and they jostled to get in line.

"Oh, man, we should have organized this better," another elf-clad woman said to Kelly. She put her fingers to her lips and whistled. "Okay! All kids get in line here, and no pushing. Santa's watching!" She gestured to the side, where Kelly had pulled up a stool and was sitting with the sweater-clad greyhound beside her. "If anybody feels a little nervous about visiting Santa, you can stop and see his reindeer, Pokey."

"Oh, right!" Kelly rummaged in her purse

and pulled out a pair of antlers, which she fitted onto Pokey's skinny head.

Zinnia laughed and pointed. "Sit by Pokey."

Glad that Zinnia wasn't tugging toward the front of the Santa line, Alec brought her over to where Kelly and Pokey sat. A couple of kids and parents were already standing nearby, and Kelly was telling the kids about Pokey. Zinnia sank down onto her knees, listening.

"Alec Wilkins, right?" One of the women in an elf costume—he saw now that there were three of them helping Santa—came over. "I remember you from high school."

"Olivia?" he guessed, and she smiled.

"Yep. I was in Kelly's grade, but everybody knew you."

"For better or worse." He'd been a good athlete, but he'd also made some trouble.

She laughed, seeming to acknowledge what he meant without judging. "Are you in town for a while?"

"Hoping to be. I'm looking for a place to stay."

She frowned and nodded toward Zinnia. "With your daughter?"

"Uh-huh, so a little hotel room wouldn't be ideal. Know of any short-term rentals?"

She shook her head. "There are a couple of Airbnbs, but they're rented out for the holidays. Where are you staying now?"

"At the Baldwins' river house."

She lifted an eyebrow. "With Kelly?"

"Accidentally, yes." He shrugged. "Long story, and it's temporary." He looked over to check on Zinnia and saw that she was sitting contentedly on the floor beside Kelly and Pokey. He winced when he saw the way the other little girls were dressed. "Guess Zinnia needs a Christmas dress, huh?"

Olivia waved a hand. "Anything goes. Hey, you're not…you weren't still with Chelsea, were you? I mean, I know you dated in high school, but you guys didn't get married or anything, did you?"

He shook his head, his gut clenching. Was she going to ask if Zinnia was Chelsea's daughter? He'd committed to concealing that, but it wasn't going to be easy if someone asked him directly. "We went different directions after high school."

"Then you've heard she died?"

This is bound to happen here. Get used to it. "I did. Very sad."

"It was. But Chelsea was bad news. She left a lot of hard feelings in town. Kelly is a much nicer person." She shook her head. "Listen to me, gossiping and speaking ill of the dead. I'm sorry. I'd better go do my elf duties." She walked over toward Santa.

Zinnia was still in the small circle of kids

surrounding Kelly and Pokey. She looked enthralled.

Alec sat down on a wooden bench behind Kelly and Zinnia. He'd known it could happen, here in Holiday Point. People were going to mention Chelsea and connect him with her.

He'd known it, but actually living it would take some getting used to.

His brother Fiscus appeared to be doing a respectable job as Santa, talking and laughing with the kids. As Alec watched the proceedings, Fiscus glanced up and saw him. A confused expression crossed his face, and then he smiled.

Surprisingly, Alec felt excited to talk with his brother. Out of the four of them, Fiscus had been the biggest troublemaker. It would be great to know that he'd pulled himself together and was working and making a contribution to the community.

Alec, the oldest, had benefited from the structure of athletics and the military. He hadn't been a Boy Scout by anyone's measure, but he'd graduated, avoided a police record, and learned to make a living.

"I thought you went for pretty women." A woman sat down next to him, just a little too close for comfort. It was the woman in the bright sweater, and she was speaking in a quiet voice that wasn't quiet enough. "Hi, I'm Tonya

Mitford. I was a couple years behind you, but I knew you dated Chelsea Walsh in school, right? I'm surprised you're with Kelly now."

He saw Kelly's back stiffen. At the same moment, he saw one corner of Tonya-the-sweater-woman's mouth quirk up. She'd done that on purpose.

Just like before, he felt an urge to protect Kelly. "Kelly's such a classy lady," he said to Tonya, not even glancing at her tight green sweater and skinny jeans. Instead, he smiled in Kelly's direction. "Doesn't flaunt her looks or talk behind people's backs. I like that about her."

Someone nearby covered a chuckle with a cough.

Tonya gave him a sour look and went to stand with a couple of women she knew.

Kelly looked over her shoulder at him and raised an eyebrow. Was she upset with him, or was that sparkle in her eyes made of laughter? "Could you run out to the truck and get Pokey's treat bag?" she asked. "It's on the front seat."

"Sure thing." He looked at Zinnia. "Want to come with Daddy?"

"Stay with Miss Kelly," Zinnia said, leaning against Kelly's arm.

He heard a little murmur. From the corner of his eye, he could tell that a number of people, including Tonya, were watching.

He was pretty sure that he and Kelly had just become a couple in the eyes of Holiday Point.

To his surprise, the thought didn't bother him.

Oh, there was no way he and Kelly could be a real couple. Not when he'd promised her sister never to reveal that she was Zinnia's mother. Beyond that, there was his own family with its problems. They were quite a bit different from Kelly's upstanding family. Not a good match on any level.

But that protective urge he'd felt when sweater woman had said her mean comment purposely loud enough for Kelly to overhear? That had been strong. That had felt good. Surprisingly good.

As he started to leave to get the treat bag, he heard a commotion and turned back. Two men, one a police officer and one probably a dad, were talking to Fiscus. The officer took his brother's arm, but Fiscus yanked it away, stood, and stomped off toward the back of the vendors' area.

The crowd was murmuring. A couple of kids in the Santa line started crying.

Alec left the building and walked around behind it, waiting. Sure enough, five minutes later, Fiscus came out. He was wearing street clothes and looking angry.

"Hey," Alec said quietly.

Fiscus looked up. "They kicked me out. Said I'd been drinking."

"Were you?"

"I had a couple shots, okay? Put me in a better mood for all the whiny kids."

By now, Alec was close enough to smell the alcohol. He hated that his brother had let people down, that he hadn't lived up to the commitment he'd made. It was what their family was known for.

It was a reputation Alec was trying hard to break.

But there was no point in lecturing someone who was intoxicated. "You shouldn't drive."

Fiscus let out a disgusted snort. "Can't. Lost my license. I'll head over to a buddy's, get a ride." He studied Alec. "You with that other Walsh girl now?"

"No. We're friends."

"Spare fifty bucks?"

It shouldn't surprise Alec that his brother asked for money instead of asking how he was doing, why he was in town, what was going on in his life. They'd only been in sporadic touch since Alec had left Holiday Point. It was as much Alec's fault as Fiscus's that they weren't close.

Alec reached for his wallet and pulled out a twenty. "It's not fifty, but it's something. Buy a meal, not booze, okay? Do they have another Santa in there?"

Fiscus waved a hand. "They'll find someone. Guys falling all over themselves to help out. Thanks." He took the money and walked off.

Alec blew out a sigh as he got the treat bag Kelly had requested.

Holiday Point was a good place, a family place. It could be perfect for Zinnia.

As long as his family's reputation, and her mother's, didn't attach themselves to her.

Chapter Three

As the substitute Santa waved to the few remaining kids, Kelly stretched her back and shoulders. Pokey nosed her, and she rubbed the dog's sides and gave her a treat.

Her friend Olivia flopped down on the bench beside her, still in her elf costume. "That was exhausting. Good thing Ralph Jefferson was willing to step in as Santa."

"Do you think the kids noticed it wasn't the same guy?"

Olivia shook her head. "With the beard and hair and hat, I think we got away with it. But what on earth was Fiscus thinking, coming in with alcohol on his breath at ten in the morning?"

"It's too bad." Kelly looked over to where Alec stood talking to the father of one of her first graders. Zinnia and Marie, the man's daughter, knelt by a collection of antique trucks and cars.

Alec hadn't mentioned his brother when he'd come back with Pokey's treats. He'd stayed and helped out with the kids who'd come to see Pokey. Zinnia had been a help, too, surprisingly, trying to comfort a couple of teary-eyed, frightened kids her age and telling them that Santa was nice.

"What happened to Fiscus must have been embarrassing for Alec," Olivia said. "I hear he's staying with you at the Baldwins' place?"

"Uh-oh." Kelly looked at her friend, dismayed. "Is word about that already out?"

"I don't know if word is out, but Alec told me himself. Said it was accidental and temporary."

"Right." She explained what had happened.

"Sounds like a Hallmark movie waiting to happen," Olivia said, waggling her eyebrows. "Hot guy returns to his hometown and hits it off with a local girl."

Kelly snickered. "Yeah, right. The ugly duckling whose sister he used to date."

"I'm gonna smack you for calling yourself an ugly duckling. You're pretty and sweet."

"Thanks, pal." She thought of what Alec had called her: classy. She stifled the small part of herself that wanted to be gorgeous and sought-after, not classy. It had been fun to see the way his remarks had infuriated Tonya, but Tonya had always been a mean girl and would find a way to exact revenge.

Alec and Zinnia headed toward them and Olivia snapped her fingers. "I just got an idea. Hey, Alec. Are you working while you're in town?"

"Not yet. If everything goes well here, I'll be job-hunting after the holidays."

"How would you like a temporary job? You and Kelly seem to be a good team with Pokey. She's going to be doing some visits to our day care, and we have a little grant funding left over. A male influence would be great for the kids. You should come with her on her visits. We could pay you."

Kelly stared at her friend. What was Olivia thinking?

"You could bring your daughter. She'd fit right in."

Alec's eyebrows lifted. "I'm surprised you'd offer me work after what happened with Fiscus." He nodded toward the empty Santa throne.

"You're not your brother," both Kelly and Olivia said at nearly the same time.

He smiled in a way that was almost shy. "That's true. And I'm in no position to turn down a paying job, but what do you think about it?" He looked at Kelly.

What did she think? Her world seemed to be tilting on its axis, turning her solitary Christmas vacation into a completely different thing.

Turning her worries about being perceived as a pathetic jilted bride into worries that she'd appear to have started up a Christmastime romance with the new guy in town.

But that was silly. "If you want to do it, I'm fine with it. In fact, since my car's still stuck in a snowbank, it might be nice to have a ride to some of the more remote places."

"Great. I'll double-check with my supervisor and give you a call." Olivia took Alec's number and then went off to help the other elves clean up.

Kelly started gathering her things. "I can get Olivia to drive me around to my deliveries if you and Zinnia want to get home," she said to Alec.

"We're fine to drive you. And we can talk about this therapy dog team thing. I don't want to butt into your work, and I don't know anything about therapy dogs."

"Sure, we'll talk. I think it'll be fine, but there's still time to say no if we decide it won't work. Ready to go?"

He went over to where Zinnia was playing and swung her into his arms. Kelly fell into step beside him, Pokey trailing a little behind. "Therapy visits wear her out," she said, nodding back toward the dog. "She'll sleep all afternoon once we get home."

"Pretty sure Zinnia will, too." Indeed, the child's eyes were drifting shut.

Kelly spotted Tonya talking to a couple of older women in the coffee shop section. All three stepped out into the aisle where he and Kelly were about to pass.

"I was just saying to the ladies," Tonya said, "how nice it is that you found a new boyfriend so quickly after your breakup."

One of the other women, whom Kelly knew vaguely from church, raised an eyebrow. "Although we do have to think about your influence on the children," she said.

Alec stopped and turned, his expression looked dangerous.

Kelly had no intention of being shamed for something she hadn't done. She raised a hand before he could speak. "I'm sure you don't mean to judge without knowing the whole story," she said to the church lady. She ignored Tonya, who most certainly *did* intend to judge. Or more realistically, intended to hurt. "Right now, I have some errands to do, so I can't stop to chat."

"Very domestic, doing errands together," Tonya said, flipping her hair.

"Let's go," Kelly said to Alec. "Now."

He glared at the women and then turned toward the door with Kelly.

They walked outside into lightly falling snow.

Great. More snow meant it would be harder to get someone to come fix her car, or at least, help her tow it out of the snowdrift.

But that wasn't her biggest problem.

Mrs. Overton had been ridiculous, making hints about her being a bad influence in this day and age. But they lived in a small town, and word about Kelly and Alec staying together at the river house would spread quickly. Other people would think the same thing Tonya had blurted out: that Kelly had jumped quickly into a new relationship. A live-in one at that. It was the last thing she'd do, and her true friends knew it, but not everyone was a friend.

If a bunch of rumors about her got generated, it could hurt the kids she taught. That wasn't okay.

It looked like she wasn't going to be able to stay at the river house. At the same time, spending a morning in the center of town and subject to everyone's interpretation of her life made her long to keep a little distance.

Was there a way to solve this puzzle and make it through the holidays?

Alec pulled the car out of the driveway of a small house at the edge of Holiday Point. "Where to next?" he asked Kelly, who was tucking an envelope of money into her purse.

"That's the last delivery," she said. "We can head back to the river house. Unless…"

"What?" He turned onto Main Street. Even though it was only midafternoon, the streetlights had come on. Most of the shops had holiday lights, too, and with the light snow that continued to fall, the place looked like a Christmas painting.

"Would you mind making a quick stop at my parents' place? I need to drop something off."

Alec froze.

The last time he'd been to her parents' house had been during high school years, picking up Chelsea. How could he go back there with Zinnia and avoid blurting out that Zinnia was Chelsea's daughter? That she was Mr. and Mrs. Walsh's granddaughter?

Kelly must have read something of his feelings because she waved a hand. "It's okay if you can't. I've taken enough advantage of your generosity today."

He needed to man up and face what it was going to be like to live in Holiday Point. "No, it's fine. I mean, you got me a job, after all. We can stop." Hopefully, it would just be a quick visit. She'd run inside and back out and he could put off, for a little longer, facing her parents. Her parents who'd lost a daughter they had loved, despite everything.

Her parents, who were Zinnia's grandparents but didn't know it.

He turned down the familiar road and memories flooded him. Picking Chelsea up for a summer afternoon swim in the river. Bringing her home after an evening at a forbidden party. Throwing pebbles at her window to get her to sneak out late at night.

Sadness gripped him. Back then, her troubles had been minor, a tendency to defy her parents that wasn't all that different from what a lot of teens did. If only she'd turned it around during high school, she might still be here to raise Zinnia and raise her well.

If only he'd helped her turn it around instead of contributing to her delinquency.

He pulled into the driveway of the little white house. It looked a little shabbier than it had back then. There were two old vehicles, a truck and a car, in the driveway, along with a newer-looking SUV.

He'd get through this, and then he'd focus on finding himself and Zinnia another place to stay. After multiple people had seen them driving around together, after the morning at the Santa event, word would get out that they were a couple.

He glanced over at Kelly, who was gathering

her things. She was a sweet person and didn't deserve to have gossip swirling around her.

She got out of the car and leaned back in. "Would you like to come in?"

"I'll wait here." He gestured toward the back seat as an excuse. "Keep an eye on them."

But Pokey let out a sharp bark, then a series of them, and that woke Zinnia up.

"Come in," Kelly urged. "We won't stay long."

Zinnia was screwing up her face for a good cry. Pokey was clawing at the door.

He sighed and got out. As he leaned into the back seat to unbuckle Zinnia, Kelly got Pokey out the other side. "I'm sorry," she said. "This day has been a lot. I owe you."

"It's okay. It's been fun for Zinnia." He pulled the child into his arms and she snuggled close. For a moment he forgot everything else except his beautiful daughter. What a blessing that he'd learned of her existence, that he could know her and raise her.

She lay her cheek against his chest, and determination rose in him. He was going to make sure that she had the best life he could possibly provide. He'd seen today how supportive Holiday Point could be, and he wanted to stay here; but he'd also seen the issues. His brother's drinking, gossip about him and Kelly staying in the same house, the risk of people guessing that Zinnia was Chelsea's child…he had to figure all of it out, figure out the best way to manage.

They entered the modest house. Not much had changed. The same slipcovered couch, upholstered rocker and small television. An entire corner cupboard was full of family photos, including a large one of Chelsea at preschool age, wearing a fancy dress and a tiara, with a trophy in her hands. Alec remembered hearing that Chelsea had been a star on the child-beauty-pageant circuit, until finances and Chelsea's snarky attitude had ended her run of victories. Alec was pretty sure the family had learned their lesson with Chelsea and hadn't subjected Kelly to the strain of pageant life.

"Of course we remember Alec," Kelly's mom was saying. Her eyes went shiny with tears. "I don't know if you were in touch with Chelsea after leaving town…did you know she passed away?"

His heart pounded hard in his chest as he tried to avoid thinking of exactly how well he knew about Chelsea's death. He nodded. "I'm sorry for your loss," he said, his voice a little choked.

"It was a loss for all of us." Kelly's mom hugged him. Her father reached around her to shake his hand.

There was another woman in the house, sporting white hair cropped short and a bright purple shirt and glasses. She came forward, hand extended, and greeted Alec. "I'm Kelly's great-aunt Eldora," she said. "Don't think I've met you. I made my escape from the senior lockup to visit today."

"Aunt Eldora!" Kelly shrieked, and pulled the woman into her arms. "I'm so glad you're here!" She turned to Alec, her arm still around her aunt. "Don't worry, she's not really in lockup. She lives in a perfectly nice senior apartment over on 986."

It sounded like it was the same senior community where his gram lived, although Gram was in a room rather than an apartment. He opened his mouth to say so.

"It's a prison to me," Eldora said before he could speak. "Can't stand being around all those old people."

Alec grinned. The woman had to be at least eighty herself, but she had style and sass and energy. Come to think of it, his gram sometimes complained about her neighbors when he called her.

"I'll hold the little one." Eldora sat down in a rocking chair and looked at him expectantly.

"She might be a little cranky," Alec warned.

"Same here. We'll get along fine." She held

out her arms, and Alec put Zinnia carefully onto her lap.

Zinnia screwed up her face to cry, but Eldora shook a beaded necklace in front of her, distracting her and making her giggle and grab for it.

"Aunt Eldora was a social worker in New York City for years," Kelly explained. "She's good with kids."

Clearly, this wasn't going to be the in-and-out visit Kelly had promised. Alec accepted the offer of a cup of tea and sat down on the faded couch.

He'd liked driving Kelly around. She was a sunny person, pleasant to be with. A good person, too; she was obviously trying to make money with her baking, but she'd also dropped off a big box of cookies for a family that was living in a shabby trailer. She hadn't put any money into her envelope after that visit.

"Where are you staying, Alec? With your family?" Mr. Walsh asked.

"No." He looked at Kelly, not sure how much she wanted to reveal to her family.

"Funny thing," Kelly said. "At the moment, we're staying at the river house together."

Mr. Walsh's eyebrows shot up to his hairline, and everyone else looked surprised, too.

"Mix-up," Alec said quickly. "The Baldwins

have always let me stay there when I'm in town, and I didn't realize Kelly was housesitting. I would have made other arrangements."

"That's not, well, it's not ideal." Mrs. Walsh sounded worried. "Kelly, you'd better move back here. Although Dad has the apartment half painted already…"

"I'm going to move out of the river house," Alec volunteered. "I could tell after today that it was going to be an issue, that people would talk."

"You can't move out, not with Zinnia," Kelly protested. "You need space."

"So do you, with your baking enterprise. And you're a local teacher. For us to be living there together, even by accident, will hurt your reputation."

There was a moment's silence that was a tacit acknowledgment: what Alec had said was true.

The doorbell rang. Mr. Walsh went to answer it and a moment later returned with two boxes of pizza. "Who ordered this? Guy said it was already paid for."

"I did," Kelly's aunt Eldora said. "I wanted to make a contribution to our little party. Didn't look like you had too much in the fridge." She gave Kelly a meaningful look.

They all moved to the table, and in the process of getting plates and drinks, Alec noticed that Kelly had put her envelope of money on the kitchen counter.

"No, honey, keep your money," Mrs. Walsh said in a low voice.

"Nope. It's for you." Kelly ignored her mother's protests and started carrying plates to the table.

They prayed and passed around the pizza. Alec cut Zinnia's slice into small squares. The kid was way too familiar with pizza and loved it.

"You know," Eldora said, "I've been thinking about your river house situation."

"Uh-oh. Look out when she has that expression on her face," Kelly's dad said.

Eldora ignored him. "What you need is a chaperone. I hate the retirement apartments at Christmas. If I come stay with you, no one will dare think there are any shenanigans going on there."

Everyone stared at her.

"It makes sense," she went on. "I like kids, I'll help with the baking. It's a huge place, so we can all have our privacy."

There was a moment of quiet. Then Kelly's mother wrinkled her nose. "It *would* silence the gossip," she said.

"Not that we should listen to gossip," her father added, "but you're right."

Kelly threw her arms around Eldora. "Thank you so much! That'll be perfect!"

Alec thanked her as well. But inside, he was not so sure.

To have another family member stay with them meant that he would be even more deeply enmeshed in Chelsea's family. He was also keeping a major secret from them.

This could be a disaster.

Chapter Four

The next day, after church, Kelly lifted a suitcase from the back of Aunt Eldora's SUV and carried it into the river house. Alec followed, holding a vinyl bin. Zinnia trotted along beside him, adorable in her little pink coat and boots.

Aunt Eldora was already standing in the kitchen, an open box on the table in front of her. "I intend to earn my keep by cooking some meals for you. For us. Brought a set of pans and a few ingredients."

Kelly pictured meals around the table with Alec, Zinnia and Eldora. That seemed just a little too cozy.

"No need for you to do that," Alec said. He must have been imagining the same thing, thinking it wasn't what he wanted.

"Nonsense. None of us has the means to eat out every meal, I suspect, and fast food isn't healthy. You're getting dinner cooked for you, at least most nights."

"She's stubborn," Kelly told Alec. "I've never been able to talk her out of something she wants to do."

"It's settled," Eldora said. "Now, where should I put the rest of my things?"

"Do you want a room on the first floor?" Kelly asked. "There's one bedroom down here. It's small, but cute and cozy with a bathroom next door. Or you can have a bigger room upstairs."

"I'd be grateful for the first floor. The two of you are upstairs?"

Kelly's face heated. "The three of us, yes. Alec and Zinnia are in a little suite at one end of the hall and my room is at the other end." Then she felt embarrassed that she'd said so much, as if she had to explain.

She just wanted to get this whole house situation settled. Get everyone moved in, and get it to where they were all on a friendly basis, with no undercurrents.

She led the way through the big open-plan den toward the small bedroom. She set the box down and then came back out when she heard Eldora and Alec laughing.

Eldora was gesturing at the huge moose head over the fireplace. "I'll never feel afraid with this guy here to protect me," she said. "We should give him a name."

"Brownie," Zinnia suggested, only she said it "Bwownie."

Alec winced.

Eldora looked thoughtfully from Alec to Zinnia. "Did you know someone named Brownie?" she asked the little girl.

"Bwownie was my kitty," she said. "She ran away."

Ouch. For this little girl to have lost a cat, on top of losing her mother, seemed doubly unfair.

Alec cleared his throat. "We think Brownie went to live with her brother and sister at the neighbor's house, remember?"

"Yes." The child frowned. "I tried to visit but Mommy said no."

Alec blew out a breath. "Mommy was being careful."

Zinnia stuck out her lower lip and her brow creased.

"Would you like to help me unpack?" Eldora asked the child. "I have a lot of pretty jewelry, and I need someone to help me put it away."

Zinnia brightened. "Okay!" She followed the older woman into the small bedroom.

Alec set down his box just outside the bedroom door. He stood up slowly and stared down at it for a few seconds before turning back in her direction.

His forehead was creased, his eyes sad. Kelly's curious questions died on her lips.

Obviously, there was a complicated history in his and Zinnia's lives. What had happened to Zinnia's mom? What was Alec's relationship to her?

"Guess I should move the rest of our stuff in," Alec said, "now that Eldora has chosen a room. I just have a couple more boxes."

"Sure. I can help."

"You don't need to do that."

"I can. I'll be glad when we're all settled in."

"I get that," he said. "I'm a creature of routine, too." He smiled at her, and she smiled back, and Kelly felt a little *zing* of interest. For him? From him? Maybe both.

She needed to remember that she was here to establish her man-free lifestyle, not to moon over the handsome guy who now happened to be sharing her home.

They were taking things out of the back of his truck when he touched her arm. "I should probably explain what you heard in there," he said. "Zinnia's mom had gotten into some bad habits. She...well, she had issues with substance abuse. Getting a two-month-old kitten was an impulsive decision. She couldn't take care of it. And going around knocking on people's doors wasn't safe in the neighborhood where she lived."

"Oh… That must have been hard." Since he'd brought it up, she might as well ask. "Were you two married, or…"

"No. I didn't even know about Zinnia for the first year of her life." He forked his fingers through his hair, his cheeks red with the cold. "I'm not proud to have had a casual relationship with her mother. I wish I hadn't fallen out of touch. But what's done is done." He said that last part firmly, as if to forestall questions.

Talk about not being proud of yourself. Kelly was definitely not proud of the happy feeling that washed over her, learning that he hadn't been deeply involved with, or married to, Zinnia's mom.

"I'm just glad I was able to step in when things went south for her."

"Not every man would've done that," Kelly said. "It's not easy, I'm sure, being a single dad."

"It's not. I couldn't do it without a whole lot of prayer. And I'm hoping living here will help me fill in where I can't manage, give her a fuller and happier life."

"I hope so, too." They were standing close together, their breath making clouds. "I'm happy to help any way I can. Zinnia's a sweet child."

"You've already helped us enough." Alec

looked uncomfortable. "Don't feel like you have to do more."

There was something about the way he was suddenly unable to meet her gaze. Kelly took a step back, raising her hands, palms out. "I didn't mean I wanted to intrude on your family life." She was *never* this awkward.

"I didn't mean...you're not intruding," he said. "Look, I can get the rest of this. Why don't you just take it easy?"

"Okay, sure, I will." She turned and walked back to the house, feeling like his eyes were on her.

She'd hoped that once they moved in together, everything would settle down to normal. But it hadn't. There were still strange vibes between them, and now, Kelly wondered whether things would ever feel relaxed and normal around here.

Alec was glad to get away from the river house on Sunday night. Not just because he and Zinnia could see his brother Cameron, although that was part of it. But also so he could get away from Kelly and the strange feelings he was having around her.

He needed to figure out a few things. Whether the town of Holiday Point would work for him and Zinnia, long term. Whether his brother had any leads on jobs. And how he was going to handle it when awkward questions about Zinnia's mother came up.

It hadn't occurred to him before that people would wonder. Back in Phoenix, everyone had been so busy leading their own lives that they hadn't showed any curiosity about a single man suddenly becoming a father. Of course, it hadn't been sudden, not really. He'd assumed more and more custody of Zinnia before Chelsea's death. And then there was no more mommy, and he was the full-time parent, 24/7.

Something about being here had made Zinnia open up about the early days. She'd talked about her mother several times since they'd arrived. Which was good, according to everything he'd read about child psychology. Zinnia needed to process what had happened, needed to be allowed to say whatever she wanted about her mother and her mother's death.

But that meant she'd say things that would rouse people's curiosity about her life before Alec was part of it. He needed to figure out how to punt. He definitely hadn't considered all the issues before picking up and moving here per Chelsea's wishes.

After a delicious dinner of chicken fried rice, crowded around his brother's table with his brother, his sister-in-law Jodi, and their two kids—with Jodi's emotional support dog scurrying around to scarf down the crumbs—he leaned back and patted his stomach. "Thank you. That was great."

Zinnia leaned back and patted her stomach too. "'Licious!" she said, making the adults laugh.

"She's such a sweetie," Jodi said. "We're glad you're here."

"Yeah, we are," Cameron said. "Because we're about to put you to work."

Jodi was smiling and nodding. "While the kids and I watch Christmas movies, you and Cameron are going to put up the outdoor lights. I've been bugging him to do it for weeks, and it's now or never."

"Hey, now, you know I've been busy at the shop," Cam protested. Cam had taken over an auto repair business from the owners of the property, an arrangement that allowed him to work close to home. "Making money for your Christmas gift," he added, raising his eyebrows at his wife.

"Oh, well, that's okay," Jodi said, smiling. "But we still need to get the outdoor lights done. Alec will help. Won't you?"

"Least I can do, as long as Zinnia's okay with it," he said.

"She's fine, aren't you, sweetie?" Jodi swung Zinnia up out of her booster seat and cuddled her close, and Zinnia's smile widened. "You and this little one are invited anytime. We love her already. And pretty soon, we'll give her another cousin." She patted her rounded belly.

Alec's throat tightened. That right there was why he needed to raise Zinnia near family and in a small community. He was doing his best, but he was under no illusions that he could go it alone. Zinnia needed all the love and nurturing she could get.

He helped his brother carry tools and strands of lights and an inflatable snowman out into the cold, starry night. Cameron got a ladder, and they started stringing lights along the gutter of the house.

"Any other news of the family?" he asked Cameron from the bottom of the ladder.

Cameron glanced down, his mouth twisted a little to one side. "You mean the news that's not fit for underage consumption? Dad's out on probation."

"That's…good?" He hadn't even known his father was incarcerated, though he wasn't surprised. It had happened twice before. "Is he home with Mom?"

Cameron nodded. "Hand me a couple of those screw-in hooks, would you? Yeah, he's home, and they're…okay. About the same as always."

Alec knew what that meant. But now that he had Zinnia to protect, he had new questions for his brother. "Are they involved with your kids?"

"In a limited way. I wouldn't have any of them as babysitters. Mom, Dad or Fiscus."

"Yeah." Alec thought of Kelly's family. They'd embrace being grandparents, would be reliable and loving.

But there was no use wishing for what couldn't be. "And Frank's in Florida, you said?"

Cameron adjusted the lights and climbed down the ladder. "Doing well, from what I hear. You definitely picked the wrong brother to settle near, weather-wise."

"No kidding." Alec stomped his feet to get his blood flowing. He started stringing more lights over the bushes that lined the front of the house. "How *is* Fiscus? I saw him yesterday at the Santa event." He told Cameron what had happened.

Cameron scowled. "Did he hit you up for money?"

"Yeah. Gave him twenty dollars, though he asked for fifty. Didn't want it to go to booze, and I'm not exactly rolling."

"Us either. Saving every penny to buy a bigger house of our own."

They strung lights quietly for a few minutes. "You still think it's a good place for me and Zinnia to settle, despite the family?"

"The best. And I might be able to hook you up with work. I know somebody hiring for heavy equipment repair."

"That'd be great. As soon as the holidays are past and I figure out a good day care situation for Zinnia, I'll need a job."

Cameron was on his knees in front of an outdoor outlet, squinting at it by the light of his phone. "You haven't said much about Zinnia's mom."

"I've said nothing. She's not in the picture."

Cameron glanced up. "She gave up custody?"

"In a manner of speaking."

"Is she living?"

Alec shook his head, just barely, and knelt to study the mechanism that would inflate the giant snowman.

Cameron was quiet, and when Alec looked over, his brother was standing, arms crossed.

"Look," Alec said, "I don't want to talk about her."

"I have news for you," Cameron said. "You're going to have to."

"I will, with you, someday. But there are circumstances. I can't say anything right now."

Cameron was studying him. "Is it Chelsea?"

Alec's heart dropped to his knees. He stared at his brother.

"I couldn't think of any other reason you'd conceal it or act weird about it."

"I act weird?"

"Uh-huh."

Alec felt his shoulders sag. "I don't want to

lie to people, but I promised Chelsea I'd keep that secret. And she's not around to release me from the promise so…"

"I get it." Cameron started untangling an orange electrical cord. "You and I, we keep our word. It's important when you come from a family like ours. It's just that, people will wonder. I wouldn't be surprised if Kelly's already guessed."

Alec wondered: Would that be okay if she guessed? It would be easier on him.

But if she guessed, it would put the burden of the secret on her. She'd have to worry about how to keep the identity of Zinnia's mom from spreading around the town where Chelsea had made so many enemies.

Cold flakes of snow blew into the open space between his coat collar and his hat. Through the window, he could see his daughter and her cousins all cuddled together on big pillows on the floor, watching Rudolph.

"Look," Cameron said, "for now, you just need a coherent story. Don't lie, but…say the mother was an addict and isn't involved."

"Possibly." But Alec was thrown by the fact that his brother had guessed the truth. If he did, who else would?

And what would that mean for his vulnerable daughter?

Chapter Five

Friday afternoon. The last day before Christmas vacation.

If Kelly had thought her first graders were out of control before their early dismissal, it was nothing compared to the three-year-olds in the day care classroom they'd just approached.

Beside her, Alec stared at the racing, shouting kids. Even Zinnia's mouth was frozen in a round O.

The only calm member of their group was Pokey. She sat, alert, tail wagging. The antlers Kelly had affixed to her head tilted slightly askew.

"Hi, guys!" Kelly's friend Olivia wove through screaming kids to greet them. "Sorry, it's a little loud in here. We wanted to get their energy out before you and Pokey came to visit. Hang on, let me sit them down." She put her fingers to her lips and gave a piercing whistle while simultaneously flashing the lights.

The room went silent. Twenty little faces turned instantly to Olivia for direction.

"Sit on your carpet pads." Olivia pointed. "Criss-cross applesauce."

The kids filed over to their pads and sat, cross-legged.

"She's amazing," Alec said, his voice awed. "I'd promote her to general any day."

"She'd do a good job." Kelly raised an eyebrow. "You ready to be onstage?"

"No. I'm ready to watch and learn."

Zinnia, holding his hand, started jumping up and down. "Go *in!*"

They made their way to the front of the room. Kelly had been keeping her distance from Alec and Zinnia all week, so much so that she wasn't sure whether he was trying to do the same or not. Either way, she'd missed the pair, which was absolutely ridiculous. They'd only come into each other's lives a week ago.

Eldora had cooked a couple of dinners that they'd all eaten together. Aside from that, Kelly had been busy with cookie baking and paperwork during the hours she wasn't in the classroom. She hadn't had time to think much about Alec. Which was good, because the last time they'd talked at any length, she felt like she'd been intrusive. When she'd made the impulsive offer to look after Zinnia, he'd made it clear he wasn't interested in her help.

So she'd mostly spent time in the kitchen and in her room. Occasionally, she'd heard laughter from Eldora and Zinnia, who seemed to have become instant buddies. The sound had made her smile and feel sad all at once, for reasons she didn't fully understand.

Having Alec around had added a slight twist to her plan of convincing everyone that she was a happily single woman. There had been a few raised eyebrows and a few questions about her new housemates. She'd had to clarify, several times, that she was *not* in a relationship with Alec.

They reached the front of the room. Alec sat immediately on the floor off to the side, patting an empty carpet square beside him for Zinnia. The child got a sudden case of shyness and climbed into Alec's lap instead. Kelly sat in the teacher-size rocking chair, Pokey alert beside her.

As more and more kids spotted Pokey, their decorum disintegrated.

"Pokey!"

"Pokey's here!"

"I wanna pet her!"

"Don't push!"

The surge of kids made Zinnia hide her face against Alec's chest. Alec looked like he might want to hide, too.

Olivia whistled once more, sharply, and the kids quieted down. "Let's review the rules," she said. She pointed to a series of pictures on a bulletin board, and the kids chanted.

"Quiet."

"Ask first."

"Two-finger touch."

Kelly scanned the room. While most of the kids were obviously excited and happy, one boy sat off to the side and had his knees drawn up to his chest. Tears shone on his cheeks. He looked like he might need a little extra love from Pokey.

Zinnia was peeking out from Alec's lap.

Once the rules were clear, Kelly talked briefly about how Pokey could help people who were scared or upset to relax. It was her basic spiel, not much different from the one she'd delivered to this same class the previous month. A little review didn't bother three-year-olds.

The kids lined up then, those who wanted to talk to Pokey, and each got a chance for a brief hello. Then Olivia got them started on quiet activities at their tables, assuring everyone that Pokey would stay in the classroom for the rest of the afternoon.

Once the other kids had found their seats,

Kelly gave the dog a drink and then let her chart her own course, with Kelly following close behind. Pokey went immediately to Zinnia and nudged her, and the child giggled and relaxed. "Come join the drawing group," Olivia suggested, and Zinnia said, "Pokey come." So they all went over to the table where kids were coloring. Zinnia joined in while Pokey submitted to more petting from the kids.

"Zinnia seems comfortable," Kelly said to Alec. They were both standing to the side, watching the kids draw and pet Pokey.

"She does," Alec said. "It's a good opportunity for me to check out local day cares. I'll need to enroll Zinnia somewhere after the holidays."

Soon they circulated to a group of kids looking through picture books, and another group playing with clay. That group got a few muddy-looking streaks on Pokey, but no matter. She was washable.

Next, Pokey tugged toward the little boy who'd been crying before. He sat, subdued, near a few other kids who were playing with blocks.

Kelly followed Pokey toward the boy. When the dog reached him, he didn't look up, so she stood patiently beside him. Kelly pretended to look away, not wanting to interrupt the interaction.

After a moment, the boy reached out and petted Pokey. She wagged her tail and sprawled out next to him, and his face broke into a smile.

Kelly let Pokey's leash go and backed away. A moment later, Alec walked over and sat quietly beside the boy and dog.

Olivia approached Kelly. "That's Brendon," she said quietly, "and he never talks to anybody. Especially adults. Barely makes eye contact."

"I hope Alec doesn't get his feelings hurt," Kelly said, and then laughed at herself. "I guess he can handle it, considering that he's seen combat and all."

Pokey tipped farther onto her back. Alec petted her, and then he and the boy smiled at each other.

"I love that dog," Olivia said. "She does such good work."

"She does," Kelly agreed.

Zinnia came toward her father. She was holding a stuffed dog, and she offered it to Brendon.

Alec said something—a quick word of praise, most likely—but he mostly left the conversation to the kids. Or, really, to Zinnia. Brendon didn't appear to be able to get much of a word in edgewise, but he smiled occasionally, and even laughed once.

"I want that little sweetheart in my class," Olivia said as Zinnia lay down on the floor beside Pokey, completely relaxed. "Where'd she get those social skills? From Mom?"

Kelly shrugged, although she wondered the same thing herself. "Maybe she got them from Alec," she said. "Look."

Alec and Brendon were looking through a book together. The sight of the big, rugged man with the withdrawn boy melted Kelly's heart.

"Alec would be welcome anytime, too," Olivia said. "Wow. You guys *are* a great team."

As parents started to arrive, Kelly, Alec and Zinnia said their goodbyes and headed out to the parking lot. Kelly watched Alec, covertly and thoughtfully.

He was so much more than he appeared. So much more than he used to be, which could be said of anyone, of course.

He also had his share of secrets. And Kelly was getting more and more curious about them, especially about his relationship with Zinnia's mom.

Alec pulled out of the day care parking lot and headed south. "Would you like to stop and get some dinner?"

As soon as the words were out of his mouth, he regretted them. He was already living with Kelly and working with her while trying to keep an enormous secret. What was he thinking, inviting her to socialize with him and Zinnia, too?

He risked a glance at her face.

Her forehead was wrinkled, like she was confused. "Uh, well, Eldora might expect us home."

"I told her not to cook tonight. I don't want her to feel like she has to wait on us. Only... I'm starving, and Zinnia needs dinner, too. I'd like to find a place for a quick bite, if you have time."

His hands were sweating on the steering wheel, as if he were thirteen again, asking a girl to a dance.

Which was ridiculous. He hoped she'd say no.

"Well," she said, "there are fast food restaurants all the way out on the highway, or... I know!" Her voice rose. "Food trucks! There will be at least a couple of them at the Christmas Tree Display. And there's a bonfire, and lights... it's really fun."

He couldn't think of anything he'd like better than to attend his hometown's Christmas Tree Display with her. That was concerning in itself. "They still do that?"

"It's bigger than ever. But..." She hesitated, and when she spoke again, the lilt was gone from her voice. "It might be too cold for Zinnia. Or maybe she's too tired. Or..." She broke off, and when he glanced over, he saw a flush on her face.

"Maybe you're sick of me after spending all afternoon together?" He made his tone light and joking. In reality, he hoped he was wrong.

"Oh, no! I'd love to hang out with you and Zinnia. It's just..." She trailed off.

She wanted to hang out with them. She'd *love* it.

His heart soared. "It's just what?"

She shrugged her shoulders and looked away. "I just don't want to intrude."

He saw a parking space on Main and pulled into it. Then he turned to Kelly and took her hand. "Kelly."

"Yeah?" Her one-word answer sounded breathless. Tinny music played from speakers outside the truck. In the back seat, Zinnia hummed a little tune.

"I want you to know that you're not intruding."

"Oh."

Their eyes locked together. Something, some kind of Christmas spark, seemed to pass between them.

He let go of her hand. What was it about this woman that kept drawing him, making him do things he knew were unwise? "Let's go find some food," he said roughly. He now had to get through this event he should never have invited her to. Get through it without any more of those sparks.

It was all part of checking out the community, he told himself. Making sure it was a good place for Zinnia, and for him.

They emerged from the truck, walked down to the point, and entered a wonderland of lit, heavily decorated trees lining the walkways and clustered at the center of the park. One giant tree stood at the point where the rivers came together.

A young girl stood on the stage singing "*O Holy Night*," her voice incredible, almost worthy of Broadway. There were wreaths on sale, and yard decorations. Face painting. Crafts for the whole family to make together. And people. Everyone in Holiday Point seemed to be out taking in the beauty of the decorated trees.

"Want to walk through, then grab some food and sit by the bonfire?"

"Sure." She walked along, Pokey at her side, her eyes sparkling as bright as the Christmas trees. "Look. I always like the blue tree section best."

He walked with her to it, arguing good-naturedly. "I'm a red and green guy, myself. This is a little too *nouveau*."

She raised her eyebrows. "A blue Christmas

tree is *nouveau*? I thought you were supposed to be sophisticated."

He snorted. "Not hardly." He wanted to ask her why she thought so, what she'd heard about him, but he didn't. *Keep it impersonal,* he reminded himself.

"I see we all had the same idea." Eldora came toward them, strolling along with Kelly's mom. "Gorgeous, isn't it?"

"It is."

Kelly's mom stopped and knelt in front of Zinnia. "What's your favorite tree, sweetie?"

To his surprise, Zinnia put her hands on her hips. "I like pink," she said firmly.

Kelly's mom clapped. "Me, too," she said. "And there are some pink trees here. They're down toward the river. Chelsea always liked them the best, too." Her voice sank on the last words.

Alec's heart flipped over.

"Let's go see," Kelly suggested. She hooked her elbow through her mom's and held Zinnia's hand. Eldora took Zinnia's other hand, leaving Alec to walk along behind the four females, feeling confused.

He needed to do some serious thinking and praying.

He'd wanted to find a community for Zinnia. Well, he'd found one. And watching her swing between Eldora and Kelly, he could tell she liked the attention, especially from women. Dads were great, but they weren't enough.

That need for female support would only intensify as Zinnia grew.

But how could he keep Zinnia here without having someone guess the truth about her mother? Even now, she was displaying traits that linked her to Chelsea. She was connecting naturally with her aunt, her great-aunt and her grandmother.

All of whom were smart women. What were the odds they wouldn't figure out the truth?

Chapter Six

"I can't believe you bought a pink tree!" Kelly had been busy with baking all of Saturday morning, and when she came into the front room, there it was: a six-foot artificial tree with shimmery pink and silver needles.

Alec and Zinnia had left the house early this morning and returned with several bags and boxes. Now, Alec was adjusting the branches while Zinnia tried to help. She tugged at the branches like her father was, nearly pulling the tree over.

"Come here, honey," Eldora said, taking Zinnia's hand and leading her to an armchair. Eldora picked up one of Zinnia's many stuffed animals before sitting down and gesturing for Zinnia to sit on her lap. "Let's sit with Mr. Bear and watch Daddy fix the tree," she suggested.

"His name is Bruno," Zinnia said. She

climbed into Eldora's lap and sat the bear on her own lap. "Sit still," she scolded him sternly.

Eldora smiled at Kelly. "Isn't the tree pretty? I never saw such a thing, except on the internet, but I like it."

"It's definitely nontraditional," Kelly said.

A kids' Christmas movie played on the television, the sound low. Kelly set her plate of cookies down on the coffee table. "Just in case anyone needs some fuel."

Pokey roused herself from her spot in front of the fireplace and walked toward the cookies. Kelly quickly moved them to a bookcase shelf out of the greyhound's reach.

"Cookies!" Zinnia flung aside Bruno the bear, climbed out of Eldora's lap, and rushed over.

Keeping the cookies out of the little girl's reach probably wasn't a bad idea. "You may have one, if Dad says it's okay," she said.

"It's okay as long as she brings one to Dad, too," Alec said, flashing Kelly a smile. He backed away from the tree and studied it, looking rueful. "I wanted to get an ordinary green tree, but…it's hard to deny Zinnia what she wants."

"On *sale*!" Zinnia shouted. She grabbed two cookies off the plate Kelly was holding and took one to Alec. It crumbled a little in her hand, but he ate it anyway.

Eldora and Kelly looked at each other and laughed. "Were there a *lot* of pink trees at the store?" Eldora asked Zinnia. To Kelly she added, "They may have overestimated people's interest in nontraditional trees."

Kelly laughed. "Sounds like it worked in Alec's favor."

"A *lot of pink ones*!" Zinnia spread her arms wide.

Kelly set the cookies back on the high shelf and then sat down on the couch. This was nice. She'd anticipated a solitary Christmas, hadn't planned to decorate, but here she was in a multigenerational scene that could have been part of a Christmas movie.

Alec came over and took another cookie. "Thanks, Kelly, these are great."

"More, more!" Zinnia stood on tiptoes, trying to reach the cookies.

"One more." Alec handed her one, then came over to the couch and sat down beside Kelly, close enough that she could feel the warmth of his leg. Zinnia immediately climbed into his lap.

Well, this was cozy. So cozy that Kelly felt a little out of breath. "You know," she said, trying for a detached tone, "you're going to have to decorate it, now that it's set up."

"I got ornaments." He pointed to a small bag sitting on the floor.

Zinnia climbed down and ran to the bag. She came back with one box of twelve silver balls.

Kelly and Eldora looked at each other.

"You may need a few more," Eldora said. "Thankfully, I'm pretty good at making ornaments."

Kelly snapped her fingers. "I have some art supplies in my car that I bought for school. Maybe even some pink and white ribbon."

"You ladies are the best." Alec held up the box and looked from it to the tree. "I underestimated the size of the job. I never really decorated a tree before."

"Never?" Kelly asked.

He shook his head. "I never volunteered for that job, in the army."

Zinnia was back in Alec's lap. She stuck her thumb in her mouth and leaned against his chest.

"Lunchtime for me," Eldora said. "Anyone else hungry?"

"I've been snacking on cookies all morning," Kelly said. It was a hazard of her baking hustle, and she'd already resigned herself to gaining a couple of pounds over the holidays.

"Zinnia and I got a fast food brunch," Alec said. "I think she might need a little rest now."

"No nap," Zinnia protested groggily.

"No nap," Alec agreed. "You can just lie down for a little bit."

"With Pokey," she said.

Kelly grabbed a couple of throw blankets and put them on the floor in front of the fireplace, next to Pokey. Alec carried the little girl over and set her down. He grabbed a pillow to tuck under her head and brushed back a stray curl.

"Love ooo, Daddy," she said, her voice sleepy.

"Love you too, sweetie."

Kelly's throat tightened. There was something about a father and a little girl. Alec had been a bad boy when they'd been younger, wild and careless. Fatherhood had obviously changed him. Kelly was starting to really like the man he'd become.

Unfortunately, being with Alec and Zinnia was making her think about all she'd lost when her wedding was canceled. She and Danny had talked about having children. Part of his appeal had been that he loved children, being a youth pastor.

She brushed her hands together. "Let me bring those craft supplies in and we can do a little decorating," she said, keeping her voice low to avoid rousing Zinnia.

But when she came back into the room with her bin of art supplies, Alec had turned on quiet

Christmas music. "Christmas for Two," soulful and romantic, was playing.

Kelly set the bin down and sank into a chair, her throat so tight she couldn't speak. She grabbed a napkin from the holder and wiped her eyes, hoping Alec wouldn't notice.

He did, though. He came over and pulled out a chair beside her. "What's wrong?"

She shook her head and cleared her throat and tried, unsuccessfully, to laugh.

He rubbed her back with one hand, the way you'd comfort a child.

Kelly leaned toward him.

He wrapped his arms around her and gave her a quick hug, then scooted away. "Do you want me to get your aunt?"

"No." She swallowed down her feelings. "I just, we were going to have this song at our wedding."

He grabbed the phone he'd been using to play music and turned it off. "I'm sorry. That must be hard to deal with."

She shrugged. "It's not, most of the time. Just every now and then."

"Emotions are like that. Anything I can do? Another hug?"

"Sure." She didn't want to be needy, but the affection felt so good.

He pulled her to her feet and gave her a wonderful, close hug.

Kelly closed her eyes. His broad chest and strong arms seemed to offer a deep protection against all the hurts and mean things that could buffet a woman alone.

If this was the consolation for her broken engagement, she found that she liked it.

Alec hugged Kelly until he felt her relax, and then, as soon as he could, he stepped back.

Wow.

He hadn't expected hugging Kelly to feel so good.

Not only that, but he felt sympathy for her, too. What kind of a guy would arrange for a Christmas wedding, send out the invitations, and then back out?

"Thanks for understanding." Kelly turned away as soon as he let go of her. Now she was pulling spools of ribbon out of the bin she'd brought in.

Clearly, the hug hadn't affected her the same way it had affected him.

"Should we do the first part of the tree decorating now, while Zinnia's sleeping?" she asked. "It's a little too tedious for her to enjoy."

"Yeah, if you don't mind telling me what to do." He had no idea how to decorate a Christmas tree. Coming from a family of rowdy boys, he hadn't been involved in the limited decorating his parents had done when he was younger. "My parents usually set up the tree on Christmas Eve, and I haven't done one since."

"One of us will need to stand on a chair." She started tugging one of the dining room chairs toward the tree, and he took it from her and set it close to the tree.

"Good. We'll start at the top and wind the ribbon around. It'll go faster with two of us doing it."

In the end, she stood on the chair and he stood beside her, tall enough to reach to the top of the tree. She tied a ribbon to the top and then passed it over to him, and coached him on how to wind it around so it looked pretty.

He could smell something spicy on her. Was that from baking cookies, or perfume, or just her own unique fragrance?

He shouldn't think that way about the sweet woman he happened to be sharing a house with. Who'd been kind enough to include him and Zinnia in her therapy dog work so he could make a little money and Zinnia could meet local kids.

Who also happened to be Chelsea's little sister.

And that right there was the problem. He

needed to keep Chelsea—or rather his promise to conceal her identity as Zinnia's mother—front of mind. He had seen how poorly Chelsea was regarded in the town. If people found out Zinnia was her daughter—and since his own family didn't contribute greatly to her good reputation—he feared Zinnia would be hobbled before she'd even started to become a part of this community.

When it was his turn, he took the ribbon from Kelly and wound it behind the tree, then passed it back to her. This close, he could see the sprinkle of freckles across her nose, the natural pink of her cheeks.

He wanted to toss aside all his caution, like throwing off prison shackles, and let his feelings for Kelly flow naturally. But that wouldn't be right, and a better man would step back and keep his distance, would avoid hugging and tree decorating and laughing together with a woman he craved more than a hungry kid would crave the cookies Kelly baked.

He wasn't that great of a man, though. He was a Wilkins, from the troublesome Wilkins family, known for giving in to their impulses and following their feelings down paths headed straight for destruction. You couldn't get rid of your own blood.

He wrapped the ribbon another round and

caught a glimpse of Zinnia shifting in her little nest. Immediately, he pulled himself together.

Maybe it wouldn't be easy for him to restrain the feelings he was starting to have for Kelly, but he had a little girl to protect. There was no way he'd do something to hurt Zinnia.

Zinnia carried the same blood Alec did, blood mixed with that of Chelsea. She could end up in trouble from either side.

He let his eye travel upward to the top of the tree. He'd buy a star to put there and serve as a reminder. Following the star, following Jesus, that was the way out of the tangle of his own emotions. He wasn't doomed to repeat the errors of his parents, any more than Zinnia was.

Following Jesus probably meant stepping back from the woman who drew him like a moth to a flame, but who was forbidden to him. He secured the final stretch of ribbon to the bottom of the tree and then stepped back. "Thanks for your help," he said, "but I'm sure you have other things to do. Zinnia and I can take it from here."

The day after they decorated the Christmas tree, Kelly headed to church early. She'd promised to help Olivia, who was in charge of the children's pageant, with the main event of church services today.

Pokey trotted into the old stone building at her side, head held high. It was as if she knew she'd be serving as one of the stable animals. With her tall, thin body, Pokey was more of a natural for the reindeer role she'd played several times already. But there weren't many animals who were easy to manage and didn't mind kids, so Pokey had been chosen to serve as a very skinny cow.

Kelly and Pokey got to the entrance of the sanctuary and were immediately attacked by overexcited kids. Kelly gave hugs and encouraged quiet, or at least gentle, behavior for Pokey's sake.

"Thanks for being willing to help." Olivia's face was flushed, her hair coming out of its messy bun. "If you can just keep some of them busy with Pokey, I can get the latecomers coached and ready to go."

"Sure thing." Kelly was glad to have a job this morning. It took her mind off yesterday's weirdness.

She'd loved spending time with Alec and Zinnia and Eldora. It had fed something deep in her soul, a need she'd tried without success to shove aside.

Okay, she'd been wrong about her choice of fiancé. Twice. But in large part, that was because she'd so wanted to marry and start a family. Decorating a home, surrounded by family, was one of the best Christmas activities she could imagine. It couldn't be replicated alone.

She'd been going along, enjoying the time together, helping Alec decorate Zinnia's pink tree. He and Zinnia and Eldora had loved her Christmas cookies. He'd been kind when she'd had an emotional moment about the song she'd intended to include at her wedding. They'd been talking and laughing together.

And then, abruptly, he'd dumped her as a decorating partner. Why?

She was self-aware enough to realize she was currently a little sensitive about being dumped in any capacity. But even putting aside her hurt feelings, she wondered what exactly had been going on. Why had his laughter stopped and his face gone expressionless? Why had he moved across the room from her, as if she'd suddenly become contagious with Christmas flu?

She almost welcomed the distraction of a scuffle near the bulletin boards. "Micah, no hitting. Josh is your friend."

"He burped in my face!" Micah protested.

"Micah, please go hold the door for Mrs. Montgomery." The widow used a wheelchair and was struggling to get through the automatically opened church doors before they closed. "Josh, I need you to very gently wipe off the little kids' hands. It looks like your sister and a couple of her friends got into some chocolate candy." She grabbed a couple of hand wipes from a strategically located container and handed them to Josh. "Go on. Now, before they mess up their Christmas clothes."

"You're a blessing," Olivia called as she hurried to corral a couple of older girls who'd started chasing each other around the entryway's Christmas tree.

Good. Kelly wanted to be a blessing. She wanted to bathe in the spirit and forget all the messy emotions she was feeling at this time of year.

Christmas was a happy time, the most joyous occasion in the church year. The birth of Jesus, the savior of the world. During church services, when they sang and listened to the readings and lit the advent candle, it was easy to focus on that.

The rest of the time, though, all kinds of other feelings got attached to the season. Between Christmas movies where everyone found love, and TV commercials where the perfect gifts were received with joy, and Christmas cards displaying happy, smiling families dressed in matching outfits, it was easy to get the feeling that your own Christmas wasn't what it should be. Social media just amplified the impression that everyone else was having a better holiday.

She knew she'd contributed by planning a Christmas wedding with all the trimmings. Now she was paying the price.

More people were streaming into the sanctuary now. Attendance was high on this last Sunday before Christmas Eve. Kelly helped Olivia herd the kids to the front of the church and get them into position.

"Look, Miss Kelly!" One of the girls she'd taught in first grade several years ago came rushing in late. "Our dog was a cow for Halloween, and I brought the costume for Pokey, since she doesn't really look like a cow."

Kelly was pleased to see that the shy first grader had turned into a more confident fourth grader. "Thanks, honey. Want to help me put it on her?"

By the time they'd slipped the black-and-white-spotted cow costume on Pokey—doubling the ties around the dog's skinny belly—the music started playing. "Watch Miss Hopkins," she urged the kids, gesturing toward Olivia. Then she retreated back to the front row. She'd be available to help if needed, and to supervise Pokey, but she wasn't part of the program and she was glad of that.

The children started to sing and Kelly sat back and let the cuteness and the music and the fragrance of pine boughs wash over her.

The kids were well-rehearsed and mostly remembered their lines, and the adult readers kept things focused with short Bible readings. Olivia had wisely included breaks for the congregation to sing some carols, taking the spotlight off the kids for a few minutes so they could regroup.

Kelly sang joyously. Yes, it was here, in church, that she felt the deep meaning of the season and the peace that went along with that.

About halfway through the performance, there was a commotion at the back of the church. A moment later, a small body propelled itself into her lap. "Daddy said I couldn't, but I can!" Zinnia shouted, her cheeks wet with tears. She climbed into Kelly's lap.

Quiet laughter and a couple of "aww" sounds came from the congregation.

Kelly cuddled Zinnia close, effectively trapping her from disrupting the children's performance. She looked back and saw Alec coming toward them, his expression thunderous. "I've got her," she mouthed, putting her thumb and forefinger together in an "okay" sign.

Looking exasperated, Alec slid into an empty pew behind them.

"Want to be in the show," Zinnia said, her lower lip thrusting out in a pout. "Want a pretty dress."

Fortunately, the kids at the front were singing

a loud song that covered up the whiny sound of Zinnia's voice.

Kelly put a finger to her lips. "You can only sit with me if you're quiet," she whispered.

Zinnia's expression stayed pouty, but she obeyed, and after a moment, she got caught up in the show.

With her arms around the little girl, Kelly felt her heart expand until it ached. What a sweet child. She hoped she could stay involved in Zinnia's life, at least peripherally, when the holidays were past.

And she had to admit, again, that she wanted kids of her own. She loved her first graders, but they of course spent the holidays with their families. Everyone did.

Kelly didn't want to spend her Christmases alone, but she was awful at picking potential partners. She rested her cheek atop Zinnia's head and let her wish for a family turn into a prayer.

It didn't seem possible for her to achieve her dream on her own. But maybe, just maybe, God could lead her toward the family she craved.

When the pageant ended, Alec thanked Kelly for helping and took Zinnia away with the promise of lunch with her cousins, Alec's brother's kids.

Kelly swallowed her hurt at his quick departure. She didn't deserve a medal for letting a child sit in her lap for half a service. Alec had his own life, his own plans. They didn't include her, nor should they.

Olivia was talking with parents, so Kelly helped make sure the children stayed close to meet their families. There were a couple of kids who were involved even though their parents didn't attend, so Kelly walked them to the back of the church and waited with them until their rides came.

Then she went back into the church to get her things and discovered Olivia crawling around in front of the pews, picking up tiny pieces of paper.

"Why did I let the kids talk me into confetti?" she moaned when she saw Kelly.

Kelly knelt to help. "Because it was like a birthday party, and you wanted them to have fun," she said.

"Pretty dumb idea, though." Tonya Mitford walked over and perched on the front pew. Today, she wasn't wearing one of her trademark tight sweaters, but an entire sweater dress, short and red and emblazoned with sparkly poinsettia decorations. It matched her over-the-knee boots and her red fingernails.

A few people still hung around the aisles,

talking. One of them, Mrs. Montgomery, rolled up toward them in her wheelchair. "Merry Christmas, ladies," she said and then turned toward Kelly. "I didn't know you had a child, dear. She looks just like you."

Kelly felt her cheeks going hot for some reason. Maybe it was the idea that she and Alec could have had a child together. "That's not my daughter. She's Zinnia Wilkins, Alec Wilkins's daughter."

"Well, she certainly loves you," Mrs. Montgomery said.

"Kelly's a teacher," Olivia broke in. "All the kids love her. Occupational hazard."

"True, that's right, I'd forgotten you were a teacher." She patted Kelly's hand and then her phone buzzed. "That's my ride. Thanks for a lovely show." She blew Olivia a kiss and rolled down the aisle.

"Do you need any help?" Kelly asked.

"No, no, I'm fine," she called over her shoulder. "You girls have fun."

"Did you plan that?" Tonya asked.

"Plan what?" Kelly slid back down to the floor and continued picking up tiny gold stars and silver snowflakes.

"Having Alec Wilkins's little girl come running up. It was *so cute.*" Tonya's voice was mocking.

Kelly bit back a sharp response. *It's church, be nice.* "Nope, that was a surprise to me. How are you doing, Tonya?"

"I'm actually doing great," Tonya said. "Seeing someone new."

"Oh, that's nice." Kelly glanced up. Didn't it occur to Tonya to help with the tedious task?

"Guess who it is?"

"You're obviously going to tell us," Olivia broke in, not bothering to hide her annoyance with Tonya.

"It's Danny!" Tonya said with a wide smile. "I'm seeing Danny! He's wonderful."

Kelly kept her face averted so Tonya wouldn't see her own shock. Danny was already seeing someone new? And it was *Tonya*?

"Treats me like a queen." Tonya used her phone's camera to check her makeup. Then she flipped her hair with her hand and studied the effect.

Kelly's heart was thumping fast. "Wow, well, I wish you the best with that."

"Oh, I know you were engaged," Tonya said, her voice dripping with fake kindness, "but Danny and I have talked about that. You just weren't right for him. Everyone makes mistakes. We're very, very happy together."

Kelly focused on the threads of the burgundy carpet. She felt like someone had rammed a rusty nail through her throat and another one through her heart.

Up until now, she'd felt like her breakup from Danny was an understandable misfortune. They'd both made a mistake, and he'd owned up to it in time to prevent a marriage that probably wouldn't have worked well. She'd taken a hit to her self-esteem, and she'd been embarrassed, but she was basically a strong person. She had known she'd get through it.

Tonya's gloating announcement changed everything.

If Danny was really dating Tonya, then she hadn't known him at all.

Were all men only concerned with how you looked, such that even a youth pastor could be swayed by a woman in a tight dress?

Any sense that she could ever attract a man, any little fantasies she'd entertained while spending time with Alec, all of it went right into the trash along with the confetti in her hand.

Men didn't want a wholesome woman who was *such a nice girl*, like her. They wanted gorgeous. Like Tonya. Like Chelsea.

"Don't worry, Kelly," Tonya said, feigning concern. "You'll find someone."

Pokey whined a little, got to her feet and came to lean against Kelly.

"You know what, Tonya?" Olivia stood and

advanced on the other woman like a protective mama bear. "You're way out of line, bragging about a supposed relationship you have with Kelly's ex-fiancé. And in church!" She started waving her hands toward the back of the church. "Get on out of here. Shoo!"

"Don't talk to me like I'm a preschooler," Tonya said, but she did stand up. "I just thought it was better if Kelly heard it from me, rather than from some stranger."

Olivia looked around, then grabbed a shepherd's crook from the nativity scene. "Go on, get out! Now!" She waved the long wooden implement in a threatening way.

"Talk about inappropriate for church," Tonya said as she backed down the aisle.

"Speed it up." Olivia's voice was now full-on preschool teacher. She banged the crook against the side of a pew. "Hustle. Out of here."

Tonya turned and ran, as best she could in her high-heeled boots, out of the church.

Kelly pressed her hands to her face. "You just threatened Tonya Mitford with a shepherd's crook." She started to laugh.

Olivia laughed, too, as she came to sit on Kelly's other side. "Pure impulse. I've been told I have an instinct for drama."

"The look on her face…" Now Kelly was laughing so hard she couldn't stop. Every time she looked at Olivia, or thought about the way her friend had chased Tonya down the aisle of the church, she laughed harder, and soon tears were running down her face.

And then she wasn't sure whether the tears were from laughter or something else.

Olivia brought a box of tissues from behind the pulpit and handed them to Kelly. "That was totally mean and uncalled for," she said while Kelly wiped her eyes and blew her nose. "There's no way she even likes Danny. He's not her type. She's just trying to get you upset for some reason."

"But Danny must like her," Kelly croaked out.

Olivia shook her head. "He's just being a fool. Sure, she's got long hair and an amazing figure that she loves to show off, but she's ugly inside."

"Men like the outside." Kelly cleared her throat and tossed her handful of balled-up tissues in the trash bag. "And I don't have what they like."

"Oh, hon." Olivia stood and pulled her into a hug. "You're hurting, and why wouldn't you be? A broken engagement hurts. Even a broken engagement from a fiancé who's now acting like an idiot."

"Especially that. When he's chosen the town hottie over you."

Olivia hugged her tighter and then stepped

back, her hands on Kelly's shoulders. "You're a beautiful woman with a beautiful heart. And I just know that God has something wonderful in store for you. *Someone* wonderful."

Kelly shook her head. "Nope. I'm gonna live my life as a happy single woman. Like my aunt Eldora."

Olivia squeezed her shoulders and then grabbed the trash bag. "You deserve love, my friend," she said. "Come on, let's go get a greasy brunch at the Point Diner."

Kelly wasn't hungry, but she wanted to be with her friend. "I'll drop Pokey off at the river house and meet you there." A thought struck her. "What if Tonya's there?"

"If Tonya's there," Olivia said, "I'll find a broom and chase her out of the place. You know I will."

"I do. Thank you." She hugged her friend once more, then grabbed her purse, took Pokey's leash, and headed out toward her car.

She was hurt and sad and angry. But she was also touched by how Olivia had defended her. People like Tonya and, really, Danny, weren't important in her life. Olivia was solidly there for her and, God willing, always would be. As she exited the church, she offered up a quick but heartfelt prayer of thanks for her friend.

Chapter Seven

On Sunday evening, Alec pulled his truck into the line of vehicles outside the county fairground. In the distance, Christmas lights shone.

"It looks like there's a wait," Kelly said from the passenger seat. "You know, you don't have to do this. Even though Aunt Eldora basically ordered us to."

Alec grinned. The older woman definitely had strong opinions and didn't mind sharing them. She'd as much as kicked Kelly, Alec and Zinnia out of the house, telling them they needed to cheer themselves up.

He'd been determined to stay away from Kelly after getting those inappropriate feelings while decorating the tree. Even after the church service where Zinnia had run to Kelly, Alec had managed to thank her and leave, keeping it all impersonal.

And then she'd come home with her face

puffy, like she'd been crying. She'd forced a smile for him and Eldora, given Zinnia a hug and gone upstairs to her room. She'd made an effort to be sociable at the dinner table, but it was clearly forced.

His resolution to keep his distance had dissolved into thin air. He just wanted to make her feel better.

After Eldora had railroaded them into agreeing to go to the light show, Kelly had gone upstairs and changed into a red sweatshirt and a Santa hat. She'd come downstairs with a Santa hat for Zinnia, too, and his daughter had been thrilled.

Zinnia was coming to love Kelly too much, getting too attached, as evidenced by her running to Kelly for comfort in church. But that was a problem for another day. Tonight, his goal was to cheer Kelly up and make Zinnia happy.

"I'm not just doing this because of Eldora," he said. "I want to do it, and it'll be fun for Zinnia. I'm sure she's never seen anything like it."

The line moved slowly, but finally, they turned a corner and the full array of lights came into view below them.

"Pretty!" Zinnia practically screamed. "Pretty, pretty!" She started trying to unbuckle herself from her car seat.

"They *are* pretty." Kelly turned toward Zinnia. "For now, though, we have to stay in the car. Why don't you show the lights to your animals?"

Zinnia immediately started holding up the three stuffed animals she'd insisted on bringing. "Lights for C'ssmas," she told the bear. She made the bear claw at the window. "No!" she scolded severely. "Stay in the car."

As Zinnia continued showing her animals the lights and correcting them for misbehavior, the car inched forward. The pay booth was visible now, but the cars full of kids and families seemed to each require an extended discussion before moving on into the light show.

From here, Alec could see colorful animals and blocks outlined in lights. A Christmas tree made entirely of blue lights stood high above the rest of the show. Santa and his reindeer lined the side of the road, blinking in red and green and white. There were airplanes with propellers that seemed to go around and snowflakes that flashed, appearing to fall.

"What was her childhood like prior to now?" Kelly asked, her voice low.

Uh-oh. Dangerous territory. "Let's just say it wasn't full of enriching activities," he said quietly. In his heart, he begged her not to ask more questions. He was feeling tender toward Kelly. It would be hard to lie to her.

She nodded thoughtfully. Then she turned back toward Zinnia and got involved in her game of showing the animals the lights.

How had it happened, he mused, that Kelly had grown up to be such a different woman than Chelsea had been? They'd belonged to the same family, with the same set of parents, raised in the same house. They were both smart women, although Chelsea would have disagreed with that statement. She'd struggled with dyslexia, which had made school less fun and rewarding for her.

She'd been breathtakingly beautiful, the stuff models and movie stars were made of. Maybe that was the problem. She'd always gotten attention for her looks, rather than for her talents and abilities and interests. But, of course, looks weren't enough to keep friends and boyfriends. Looking back, Alec knew that he'd been bowled over by Chelsea's beauty, but quickly lost interest in spending time with her.

He should have kept that in mind when he'd come home on leave. But he'd been lonely, and not only was Chelsea beautiful, but she was a link to a happier, less complicated time. So when she'd suggested he stop in Phoenix on his way home, he'd been glad to do it. It had felt good to be in the company of a woman who smelled nice and wore pretty clothes. And he'd been shallow back then. His layover in Phoenix had been pleasant, but he hadn't minded that it was brief. Just like in high school, he and Chelsea didn't have much to talk about.

He shouldn't have done it, but he didn't regret it. God had worked it for good because he had Zinnia. He looked back at her, laughing as she held her stuffed frog to the car window, and overwhelming love filled his heart.

A car horn tooted behind him, and he realized it was his turn to pull up to the ticket booth. He waved away Kelly's money.

"You can park and walk through, or drive through," the attendant explained. "If you drive, you'll still have an opportunity to park near the end. There's a bonfire and food stands and a gift shop."

"We'll drive through," he decided, and pulled the truck forward. "Is that okay?" he asked Kelly.

"I think it's best. Some of us are a little tired." She smiled at him.

"There's a Christmas CD in the console," he said.

She dug through, found the collection of carols, and put it in. Soft music filled the car.

In addition to the more commercial parts of the display, there was a prominent Nativity scene. Kelly let out a little shriek. "Joseph moved," she said. "I think that's a living nativity."

Alec braked and squinted. "I think so, too," he said. "Is that a live donkey?"

Kelly peered through the car window. "It is!" she cried out. "Look, Zinnia, there's a real donkey."

"And lambies," Zinnia said.

"She's right!" Kelly pointed toward the display's wooden fence. Sure enough, there were two groups of lambs, one set sleeping, one set standing as if waiting to be fed. "Look, Alec, live lambs."

As he listened to her and Zinnia's excitement, he was filled with a sense of rightness. He was glad they'd come.

They were about halfway through the display when there was some sort of holdup. Alec glanced into the back seat, worried that when Zinnia realized they'd stopped, she would get upset and start to cry. It was getting close to her bedtime.

But no worries. She had her animals clutched to her chest and her eyes were blinking closed. "She'll be out in five," he predicted.

The cars still weren't moving, so he put the truck in Park. "You seemed upset when you came home this afternoon," he said to Kelly.

"I wasn't… Well, you're right. I was upset." She paused, drew in a breath, and let it out in an audible sigh. "Danny, my ex-fiancé, is seeing Tonya."

"Who's Tonya?"

"That woman who wears tight sweaters. Who was being mean at the Christmas market."

"Oh. That Tonya." He'd noticed her in church. Most likely, everyone had. That had to be the intent behind her totally inappropriate outfit. "Wait, *your* ex is dating *her*? Are you sure?"

"She told me so," Kelly said, her voice glum. "Guess he's moving up in the world."

"You're joking, right?" He stared at her. "No man with any sense would consider her a step up from you." Women like that, who displayed their bodies for anyone and everyone to see, didn't appeal to him. Even when he was younger, he'd felt the same way. And then there was the matter of her personality. "All I can say is, you're well rid of him."

"I am." She sighed again. "It still stings, though, you know? He's not who I thought he was. And people will think…" She broke off the sentence and looked away.

"Will think what?"

"I don't know." She spread her hands and shook her head. "That I can't keep a man? That I'm not anywhere near as pretty as she is? That he was smart to have shifted over from me to her?"

"Whoa, whoa, whoa," he said. "Don't—"

"I know, I know, I'm being a bad feminist,"

she said. "Even a bad Christian. Looks don't matter and all that. I know."

"You're a beautiful—"

Again, she interrupted. "You don't have to say that, but thanks. Wonder what's going on up there?"

It was a clear effort to change the subject, and since he didn't know how to disabuse her of her mistaken notions, he let the change happen. The line of cars started to move, slowly, veering around some obstacle at the direction of a man waving a flashlight.

As they moved forward, the reason for the holdup was visible. Several people had gathered in an area where the lights had gone out. A couple were trying to stand an object up, while others knelt beside a light board. Then a few men broke off from the group and stood, gesturing in a way that suggested an argument.

Alec saw a familiar figure in the arguing group. Fiscus.

Shame washed over him, making him feel a little sick. Everyone in town was working together to make Christmas festive and fun, except his family. As soon as he got the car past the little crowd, he pulled into a parking area. He glanced into the back seat. Zinnia was sleeping. "I'll be right back," he said to Kelly, and exited the car.

By the time he approached the cluster of people, things had disintegrated into yelling. Fiscus was the loudest, shouting back at another man who appeared to be a security guard. Both gestured toward a fallen structure on the ground.

Alec didn't know his brother all that well anymore, but he did remember the signs that indicated Fiscus was about to blow up. He waded into the group and took Fiscus by the arm. The smell of alcohol emanated from him. "Hey. Chill. Let's get you out of here."

"He's not leaving until he either fixes this or pays for it." The security guard puffed up his chest and looked around. Cars were driving by, some with the windows down, and the occupants looking out at them.

"I'll pay for it," Alec said. "But let's get the argument away from the display and the kids."

Fiscus twisted away and headed over toward a couple other guys who looked as messy and unshaven as he did. "It was an accident," he shouted.

His friends urged him toward the walking path that led to the exit.

The guard didn't stop him, so apparently no charges were going to be filed. He swung around and glared at Alec. "Who are you?"

"For better or worse," Alec said, "I'm his brother."

"Are you good for the money? Your brother wouldn't be." The man gestured in the direction Fiscus had gone.

"I'm good for it," Alec gritted out. "I keep my word." He clung to it, actually. Keeping his word defined him.

It was a way of differentiating himself from his family.

In the car, Kelly watched Alec talking to the security guard. She could tell from the set of his shoulders that he was angry, but he was holding it back. There was no more shouting.

She knew what it was like to have an embarrassing sibling. Knew that people tended to wonder if you were the same, and to blame you for things the sibling did. She felt sorry for Alec.

But she wasn't going to bring that up, talk about Chelsea, dig into his feelings about his brother. She'd already gotten way, way too open with him, telling him about Danny and about her own feelings of inadequacy. She wished she hadn't opened up like that. Men didn't like it when women got emotional. He'd thought she was seeking reassurance about her looks, and he'd started to give it, and she'd hated that. Hated the artificial compliments he'd started to bestow.

From here on out, she was going to keep things superficial.

He marched back to the car, his face set in angry lines. When he got in, Zinnia woke up and let out a fretful cry.

Kelly had a second's worry that he was going to take out his anger on the child.

Thankfully, he didn't. Of course he didn't. "Hey, it's okay," he said, leaning into the back seat and brushing a hand over his daughter's hair.

Zinnia looked at him and smiled. In the clearing next to the parking area, families were sitting on the logs surrounding a big bonfire.

His voice still gentle, he said, "Anyone want to roast some marshmallows?"

"Yeah!" Zinnia sat up straighter and reached for the buckle of her car seat.

"Okay with you?" Alec asked Kelly.

"Absolutely."

So they got Zinnia out of the car and headed over to the bonfire. They were handed a roasting stick and three small bags, each holding marshmallows, graham crackers and chocolate.

Alec impaled a couple of marshmallows on the stick and held them over the edge of the coals. "When you're bigger," he told Zinnia, "you can do this yourself."

She was sleepy enough to be pliable. "Okay, Daddy."

As Kelly watched Alec roast the marshmallows and then put the s'mores together, she realized his expression was serious and he wasn't looking anywhere but at the project and his daughter. She glanced around and noticed several people watching them. The security guard he'd been arguing with was talking to a couple of women, and gesturing toward Alec.

Poor Alec.

He handed her the finished s'mores and made more and finally they all sat on the log to eat them. Except Alec didn't eat his. He just helped Zinnia with hers and then held her close.

The security guard came over. Apparently, the conversation with the women had gotten him into a self-righteous frame of mind. "You really need to get your brother under control," he said. "There are kids here."

Kelly felt like yelling at the man. How was Alec supposed to control his brother, who was an adult with a drinking problem? Fiscus had been causing trouble in town for several years. Yet, because Alec was back, people wanted to dump that problem on him, even though he already had a lot on his plate.

"I'll talk to him," Alec said. "And I'll pay for the destruction right now." He pulled out his wallet and counted out some cash. "Will that cover it?"

"Probably." The man walked off without thanking Alec.

Alec turned toward her but didn't meet her eyes. "Ready to go?" he asked, his voice tight.

"Sure," she said. She wiped off Zinnia's mouth and Alec carried her back to the car, where she drowsily accepted being buckled into her car seat.

As they headed home, she said, "You're not your brother. You shouldn't be held responsible for him."

He shrugged. "I figured when I came back here that there might be some issues with my family."

"But you have to detach yourself emotionally. That's what I had to do with Chelsea. Otherwise, I was following her around cleaning up her messes, and that didn't help either of us."

"It's tough," he said. "Sorry you had to see that."

She reached out and took his hand. "I feel for you."

He looked over, his expression inscrutable.

She got a little lost in his eyes. And then he pulled his hand away and they drove the rest of the way home in silence. How had it happened? She'd wanted to bring things back to the surface, but in comforting him, it seemed that her heart had gotten even more involved.

* * *

After putting Zinnia to bed, Alec came downstairs, restless and out of sorts.

He *wasn't* going to use thoughts of pretty, sweet Kelly to drown out his worries about his family and their reputation in this town. Kelly had probably gone straight to bed. He was going to get lost in some mindless crime show or a Sunday night football game.

He heard her rattling around in the kitchen, though, chattering to Pokey. He stuck his head in the door, and there she was, apron tied over her clothes, mixing something up in a big bowl. "I wasn't tired," she said, half-apologetically. "So I decided to get started on some baking I need to do for tomorrow. Hope I didn't keep you up."

"I'm going to watch mindless TV," he said. "You're welcome to join me when you're done working."

She raised an eyebrow. "Thanks."

Had he been out of line, inviting her to do something with him? At the house she probably perceived as rightfully hers?

He couldn't figure it out, so he just went into the living room, turned on the TV, and started channel surfing while his mind raced.

He'd initially thought the biggest problem regarding Zinnia would the fact that she was

Chelsea's daughter, a relationship he'd committed to keeping quiet. He wasn't sure that had been the right thing to do, but he was on that road now and couldn't turn around.

Now, it turned out that Fiscus was causing trouble in town, adding shade to a family name that was already tarnished. Maybe he'd made a mistake coming here. It was great to be near his brother Cameron, and good for Zinnia to get to know her cousins, aunt and uncle. When they'd made a quick stop at the senior community to visit Gram, she'd been over the moon to meet her great granddaughter for the first time. But it was work to try to keep his secret, and work to keep the more difficult parts of his family from hurting Zinnia's reputation.

Hopefully, most people wouldn't assume that a drunk uncle had any bearing on a sweet little girl and how she should be treated. If news of who Zinnia's mother was came out, though, that could be trouble.

He looked around the snug room. The fire warming it, the pink Christmas tree, the knowledge that Eldora was asleep in the room down the hall and Zinnia asleep upstairs. And Kelly clattering around in the kitchen. All of it appealed to him at a deep level he was only starting to recognize in himself.

He didn't want to leave. Didn't want to uproot himself and Zinnia from the warmth of this nurturing environment.

He settled on an action movie and turned the volume low, then watched it unseeingly. It wasn't just that he didn't want to uproot himself and Zinnia from the coziness of this place. He also didn't want to let go of Kelly.

They'd only been here a little more than a week, so how did he feel so close to her?

Partly, it was that they'd grown up together, here in Holiday Point, had known many of the same people, had known each other at a younger age. It was easy to slip into a familiar routine with her, easy to talk with someone who shared the same background and interests.

But that wasn't all. He liked talking to Kelly. She was kind and insightful. And it seemed to him that she'd gotten a raw deal, in her family when her looks had been compared to Chelsea's, and then in the town where her broken engagement had humiliated her.

She didn't deserve that. He felt a powerful urge to protect her from any forces that were against her. That was a new feeling to him.

She came in and leaned against the back of an overstuffed chair, Pokey at her side, looking at him. "Were you serious that you wanted company? You look like you're thinking."

"Too much," he said. But looking at her as she

stood there chased his chaotic thoughts away, made him crystal clear on what he wanted. Which was for her to stay here awhile, with him. "Come sit down. Maybe you can help me focus on the TV instead of my worries."

She looked at the screen and shook her head. "Too scary for me. I'm more the cozy Christmas movie type."

He flipped channels until a heavily decorated town and two perky people showed up on the screen. "This better?"

"Much." She came and sat on the other end of the couch. She was wearing pink, slide-type slippers that gave him a glimpse of matching pink toenails. "Are you worrying about your brother?" she asked.

The movie played in the background, a pleasant splash of noise and laughter. "Yeah. I didn't consider when I came back how my family was still notorious here. How that might affect Zinnia. She's little now, but I would hate to see kids tease and laugh at her because of her uncle."

"Yeah. I get that. But…it's really just Fiscus, right? I haven't heard much about your parents in the past few years."

"That's good, considering Dad just got home from serving a jail term."

"Oh…" Sympathy crossed her face. "I'm sorry. I didn't know."

"If you didn't, most people in town didn't. And Mom's doing okay, doing call center work from home." He didn't add that they were obviously barely making it.

"Your brother Cameron seems like a great guy," she said.

"Yeah. He is." He frowned. "Fiscus could be, too, but right now…he's not."

"What's going on with him, do you think?" she asked quietly.

He shook his head. "He was in the army, had a good run, and I thought he was on the right path. Then he moved down to Atlanta for a few years and got into some trouble. Spent time with the wrong people. Apparently he had a girlfriend and kid who, well, paid the price. Got killed by some of his connections. Mom said he came back wild."

Her hand went to her mouth, her forehead wrinkling. "How awful. Who wouldn't be a complete wreck in that situation?" She paused, then asked, "Is there anything any of us can do?"

That was Kelly, kind to a fault. "Not unless he dries out."

"But…" She broke off. "Never mind. Not my business." She pressed her lips together and then burst out, "There's an AA meeting at the church where Danny's the youth pastor. Maybe if he…"

"I'll let him know if I can catch him sober."

He reached out and grasped her hand. "Thanks for being kind instead of judgmental."

She laughed, but without humor. "Believe me, I can be plenty judgmental. Let me show you something." She ran upstairs and, a moment later, trotted down with an accordion-type file folder.

On the front of it was written, *Chelsea*.

Alec's heart sank. "What's that?"

"Everything we have about Chelsea, everything we know." She opened it up and started handing things over to him without even looking at them. They were all worn, newspaper articles and case files and business letters. Someone had looked at them again and again.

There were crime blotter articles from their small-town newspaper and one about a hit-and-run. All of Chelsea's bad behavior or, at least, all that had become public knowledge. "Did you print all these out?"

"Mom did," she said. "She was getting obsessed after Chelsea died. Trying to figure out what she could have done differently, where she went wrong. Because see…" She dug through and found a couple of primary-school report cards. "Chelsea did okay in school in early years. And she even got a good citizen award." She passed over a gold construction-paper certificate.

"What *did* happen?" When he'd known Chelsea, in high school, she'd been anything but a good citizen. "Was it the dyslexia?"

"That had something to do with it. Nobody diagnosed it early on, so she was just thought to be slow to learn. She got really frustrated. By the time she got help, she already had a terrible attitude toward school." She shook her head. "But a lot of kids deal with learning disabilities and don't go off the rails." She riffled through more papers. "Bills she left unpaid, traffic citations she didn't respond to, notes requesting money and blaming Mom if she didn't give it to her." She shook her head. "Chelsea could be awful."

"Wow." He was reeling from the assessment. He also had a sinking realization that, if he'd ever thought he could pretend he hadn't told Kelly about Chelsea because it hadn't come up…well, it just had, and he'd kept silent.

"Hey, it's okay," she said, patting his arm. "I just wanted you to know you're not alone with the troublesome sibling thing."

"Thank you." He watched as she put the folder back on a shelf. "Do you…carry that with you wherever you go?"

She shook her head. "I brought it to get it away from Mom, hopefully stop her from obsessing."

"Speaking of, let's stop obsessing about our siblings, too. Want to watch that movie?"

So they turned up the sound and watched the holiday movie that was playing. Partway through, she leaned against him, and he put an arm around her.

Moments later, she was asleep.

Alec stroked her hair and didn't move even when his shoulder started to fall asleep. It was so good to have her in his arms. She was soft and sweet, her cheeks pink, her breathing regular, those year-round freckles giving her a permanently young and cute look.

She smelled like cookies.

She was a good person, too. She would be the perfect mother for Zinnia.

And where had *that* thought come from?

Kelly was Zinnia's aunt. And he was only now starting to realize that she would be a wonderful aunt and a wonderful influence on Zinnia. Her parents would be great, too.

Was Alec doing the right thing, depriving Zinnia of her family so as to keep his word to a dead woman who hadn't taken great care of her daughter in the first place?

His brain hurt with thinking, so he lowered the volume on the TV and leaned back on the couch, feet on the ottoman, Kelly snuggled against his side.

He must have fallen asleep, but he woke instantly when she stirred and sat up.

"What time is it?" she asked. Her cheeks were pink.

He looked around, saw the moon shining in through the tall windows. "I don't know. Middle of the night."

"Sorry I fell asleep on you."

He kept hold of her hand.

He couldn't stop looking at her. Her hair mussed, her face flushed. He had loved holding her. It had felt more right than anything he'd ever felt, aside from holding Zinnia. It was as if he and Kelly were meant to be together.

Their gazes tangled, and he couldn't hide the emotion in his, and her eyes darkened a little. So she knew. Did she feel it too?

There were all kinds of reasons neither of them should feel it, but it was late and the Christmas tree and fireplace shed the only light in the room, and her hair smelled like sugar and vanilla. He had the rest of his life to be reasonable.

Tonight, now, might be the only chance he had to be close with this woman who'd taken over his mind and his heart. He reached forward and brushed back a strand of her hair, letting his hand linger on her cheek.

There was awareness in her eyes. She leaned the slightest bit toward him.

It was all the invitation he needed. He pulled her close and kissed her.

Chapter Eight

Kelly had never been kissed like this before.

Alec's hands were warm on her shoulders, and his lips moved over hers with assurance. But his confidence didn't make him pushy. She knew she could end the kiss with a word or a touch.

He lifted his head and smiled down at her. "I've been thinking about doing this ever since we first arrived here."

He *had?* Kelly's heart hammered.

He touched her chin, and she closed her eyes, and he kissed her again. Gently. Tenderly.

She relaxed and drank it in, like a sweet glass of water after weeks in the desert. She wanted to stay in his strong, protective arms forever.

He kissed her closed eyelids, light butterfly kisses, and then leaned back, still holding her shoulders. She opened her eyes and looked at him. "Wow," she said.

"Yeah. Wow." He pulled her into a loose embrace, and she rested her head on his shoulder. Beneath her hand, spread on his chest, his heartbeat was strong.

This felt like home.

After a moment, a tiny doubt surfaced inside her. Could she really trust her feelings? They'd led her astray before. She wasn't especially good at choosing men and deciding on relationships.

She squeezed his bicep and then scooted back and stood. "We should both get some rest." She leaned forward and kissed his lips once more, light as a feather. Then she headed upstairs, as giddy as a teenager experiencing a first case of puppy love.

The next morning, as she made coffee and heated up breakfast rolls, Kelly still felt as though her feet were barely touching the ground. Her heart fluttered and her hands were so damp that she nearly dropped her coffee cup.

They were going shopping for Zinnia's new dress today. What would that be like? How would Alec act? How would *she* act?

Go slow, go slow, she counseled herself. Just because they'd kissed, that didn't mean they were a couple. A lot of people kissed and then moved right on, no feelings attached.

Last night had been different, though. Their

kiss had been rich with feeling, and she knew it hadn't been just on her side.

Zinnia ran into the kitchen and threw her arms around Kelly. "New dress, new dress!"

Alec followed, his step heavy and slow, dark circles under his eyes. He gave Kelly a quick smile and then went about getting breakfast for Zinnia. Eldora came in then, and they all talked together, Zinnia excited, Eldora curious about the light show last night and the shopping expedition today.

Kelly packed up cookies for a round of deliveries. Alec was quiet as he warmed up the car, then he helped her load the cookies and went back inside to get Zinnia. He settled the child in her car seat, handed her a favorite stuffed animal, and then backed out and closed the door.

As Kelly started to climb in the passenger seat, he put a hand on her arm. "Let's talk a minute," he said. He wasn't smiling.

Despite her warm coat, Kelly shivered. "Sure."

Around them, snow fell lightly on the pines that lined the river. Somewhere in the surrounding woods, a bird called out a stern *chirp-chirp-chirp*.

Alec studied her gravely. "That kiss last night shouldn't have happened. I got carried away and I apologize."

She tried to read his hooded eyes. "I felt carried away, too, in a good way."

He shook his head. "I can't be in a relationship with you. I should never have touched you. It won't happen again."

Kelly felt like someone had dropped her from a great height. The air was knocked out of her and she couldn't speak. Couldn't think.

She'd experienced something similar during Danny's breakup speech. Except…this felt worse.

She'd cared for Danny, but in a mild, almost practical way. She'd thought he would be a good husband and that they'd have a good life together.

Her feelings for Alec were a different story. Her heart had danced last night. Her feet hadn't seemed to touch the floor this morning. She'd kept pressing her fingers to her lips to convince herself that the kiss had really happened.

She'd hardly been able to believe that someone as wonderful as Alec wanted to kiss *her*.

As it turned out, he *didn't* want to. Was she a bad kisser? Or just generally unappealing, as Danny had implied?

He was looking at her with something like concern. "I hope we can still be friends," he said.

Ugh. Danny had said the exact same thing.

She forced herself to nod, but the matching smile wouldn't come.

"Do you…do you want to stay home today? I'd love to have you come shopping. I have no idea how to pick out a Christmas outfit, but I can handle it if you'd rather not go."

From inside the car, Zinnia was calling. "Go! Now!"

Kelly *didn't* want to come. She wanted to go inside and hide out in front of the fire with Pokey.

But she'd promised Zinnia she would come. She was pretty sure she'd be better than Alec at picking out a dress for a little girl.

Plus, she had to do therapy visits this week with Alec. If she suddenly stopped doing things with him, people would wonder. Speculation would grow that she'd gotten together with him and been dumped again.

Which, well, she had. But she couldn't bear it if people knew.

Couldn't bear it, actually, if Alec knew how hurt she felt. She had to convince him, and other people, and eventually herself, that there was nothing romantic in her relationship with Alec. That she was happily single. She'd fake it until she made it. "Sure," she said, putting on her first-grade-teacher enthusiasm. "I want to go."

"You're sure you're okay? I'm really sorry, Kelly."

"It's fine! You're right, it's much better to be friends."

If she said it often enough, maybe she'd start to believe it herself.

At the small department store in downtown Holiday Point, naturally, it felt like everyone she knew was there. A big Christmas sale had drawn a crowd, and lots of people seemed to be off work this week.

She needed to be clear that she wasn't in a relationship with Alec, so no one would pity her when it appeared to end.

Only, shopping with an excited little girl seemed like the ultimate relationship activity. How was she going to look like not-a-girlfriend doing something so girlfriend-like?

How was she going to avoid *feeling* like a girlfriend?

Her heart hurt. It just did.

But when you felt like that, the best thing you could do was focus on others. She'd learned that during both of her broken engagements, as well as during the painful times surrounding Chelsea's death. The way to feel better was to do something for someone else.

And the person to do for was right in front

of her, tugging at her hand. "Look at this one, Miss Kelly. It's pink!"

"It's very pretty." It was also made for a much bigger child, so Kelly steered Zinnia over to a rack of little girl dresses. Alec followed along.

Kelly ignored him. "These look like they might fit you," she said, pointing to a section of the dress rack. She pulled out a plaid dress trimmed with green ribbons and held it up to Zinnia. "Yeah, this looks about right."

Then she had to look at Alec. "Do you have a price limit?"

"No. I don't know. What do dresses cost?"

She held up the green plaid. "This is probably the middle of the range," she said, showing him the price tag. "This—" She picked up a red velvet dress trimmed with white fur and looked at the price. "This is the upper end." She handed it to him.

Alec's eyes widened. "Probably not the upper end," he said.

"I like that one," Zinnia said, running her little hand over the velvet and fur. "Pretty."

Alec didn't seem like he was going to be able to withstand a strong plea from Zinnia, so Kelly stood and skimmed the store. "We could check the sale section in the back."

"Can I help you? Oh, hi, Kelly." The sales clerk was a former teacher who'd retired and now worked part-time. "Aren't those adorable? I love children's Christmas clothes."

"Me, too. Have any of them gone on sale yet?"

"No, not until after Christmas."

"Do you have anything in pink?" Alec asked.

"Pink!" Zinnia exclaimed rapturously. "I love *pink!*"

"You know," Mrs. Cramer said thoughtfully. "We do have a couple of pink dresses on the sale rack. Who's to say they're not Christmas dresses?"

Kelly looked at Alec. "Should we take a look?"

"I want *pink!*" Zinnia said.

They walked to the back of the store and Mrs. Cramer pulled a couple of dresses from the sale rack. One was clearly a summer dress, but the other had long sleeves and a full skirt.

"I want that one!" Zinnia said.

"It doesn't look very Christmassy," Alec said.

"You know, I'm guessing they have Santa hats in pink," Kelly said. "If she wore this dress and a Santa hat, it would definitely look Christmassy."

"Great idea," Mrs. Cramer said. "Do you want her to try it on?"

Alec checked the price tag. "Yes, I surely do."

Mrs. Cramer handed the dress to Kelly. "Fitting rooms are over there," she said.

Was this Kelly's role? She looked at Alec. "Do you want to help her, or—"

"*You* help me." Zinnia tugged at Kelly's hand.

"If you don't mind," Alec said, "I'd appreciate it."

So Kelly went back to the fitting room, holding Zinnia's hand. She helped her out of her coat and overalls and pulled the dress over her head. The whole time, her heart was weeping.

She wanted a little girl of her own, to love, to buy clothes for, to help. Wanted a husband to consult about family financial decisions.

She wanted the whole package they were play-acting today, but she wasn't going to get it. Just look at how she'd misinterpreted Alec's kiss as meaning he cared, when that wasn't at all true.

She fastened the back of the dress and Zinnia twirled in front of the mirror. "Pretty! I'm pretty!"

"You sure are. Should we show Daddy?"

"Yeah!" Zinnia hurtled out of the fitting room and danced her way over to Alec. "I look pretty!"

"You do, princess." He smiled and stroked a hand over the little girl's hair, then looked up at Kelly. "Do you think this is a good one?"

"Wait one minute," Mrs. Cramer said. She went to the accessories area and came back with a pink-and-red hair ribbon. She held it to Zinnia's head. "What do you think?"

"Perfect." Kelly couldn't say more because her emotions seemed to be stuck in her throat. Zinnia looked cuter than any child she'd ever seen, and she'd seen a lot.

"She's a beautiful child," Mrs. Cramer said. "As pretty as anyone on those kid pageant shows. Have you ever thought about having her compete?"

"No," Alec said. "But thank you. She's a beautiful girl inside and out."

It was the perfect answer. But Kelly kept studying Zinnia as she twirled in her fancy dress.

She almost looked like Chelsea in the old pictures of her in pageants.

Kelly helped Zinnia change clothes while Alec paid for the dress and hair bow. When she and the little girl came out of the fitting room, Mrs. Cramer pulled Kelly aside. "I'm glad you found yourself someone new," she said. "That Danny is way too flighty."

The description made Kelly smile. "Alec and I are just friends, but thank you," she said. "And thank you for helping us find the perfect Christmas outfit for Zinnia."

They were headed out the door when a little boy shouted, "Zinnia! Uncle Alec!"

A dark-haired woman Kelly didn't know hugged Alec and then Zinnia, and then looked at Kelly with frank curiosity. "Shopping day?"

"I got a Christmas dress!" Zinnia proclaimed, tugging at the bag Alec was carrying.

"And it's going to stay in the bag for now," he said. "Your aunt and cousins can see it at church next Sunday."

"Smart dad," the woman said, and stuck out her hand to Kelly. "Hi, I'm Jodi. Married to Alec's brother, and these are my boys." She introduced them. "And in case you couldn't guess, I'm expecting." She gestured toward her rounded belly.

Kelly introduced herself. "A friend of Alec's," she said.

"I can see that." Jodi looked at her with interest. "Would you all like to come for hot chocolate with us? There's a special, two for one over at the café."

Alec squeezed Jodi's shoulder and shook his head. "We need to get home."

Zinnia started to protest.

"You have to show your dress to Miss Eldora and to Pokey," Kelly said, grateful to escape more time with the inquisitive Jodi. "We can have hot chocolate at home, though."

"Fine," Jodi said with mock upset. "Only if

you'll promise to come over for a family meal this week. How about Wednesday?"

"We'll give you a call," Alec said.

"I want to get to know your girlfriend," Jodi explained.

Alec opened his mouth to speak.

"I'm not his girlfriend," Kelly said quickly. Somehow, the words hurt less when she was the one to say them, rather than Alec.

"Oh, okay," Jodi said, raising her eyebrows. "But come anyway. See you all soon." And she was off with her two excited little boys.

Kelly watched them go, sucking in a breath and letting it out in a sigh.

Obviously, Jodi hadn't believed that Kelly and Alec weren't in a relationship. After all, she was shopping for kids' clothing with him, which is something a girlfriend would do.

What would others they'd seen in the store assume? Who would Jodi tell?

Her goal was to convince anyone who was interested that she and Alec weren't in a relationship. But she'd done just the opposite, apparently, coming shopping with him and Zinnia.

Worse than that, she'd also gotten another little piece of her heart involved, helping Zinnia choose a Christmas dress.

It was a couples activity, a family activity.

But Kelly wasn't really part of a couple, and she wasn't going to have that kind of family.

She had to start getting used to that all over again.

By the time they got home from the shopping expedition, Alec felt more exhausted than on most days he'd spent fighting for his country.

Then, at least, he'd believed wholly in what he was fighting for. Now, he was battling himself.

He couldn't stop thinking about Kelly. Last night, she'd fit perfectly in his arms. She hadn't made the first move, but she'd definitely liked kissing him. At least as important, everything they did together showed him what a wonderful person she was.

He hated that he had to hurt her. Because he *had* hurt her; he'd seen it in her eyes.

But how else could he keep his promise to his daughter's mother?

Being a man of his word meant everything to him. Even this morning, when he'd been an emotional wreck from trying to figure out what to do about Kelly, he'd pulled it together enough to check in with the Christmas light show managers to make sure they'd received his cash for the decoration Fiscus had broken.

He'd promised Chelsea to keep her identity

as Zinnia's mother a secret. And he understood her reasons for wanting that.

He couldn't break his word. But he also couldn't stop thinking of Kelly as a woman he cared for and wanted to protect.

When they pulled up at the river house, there was an unfamiliar car in the gravel driveway.

"Wonder who that is," he said to Kelly, who'd been silent throughout the ride home.

"My parents," she said. Then she pressed her lips together into a straight line.

It was his first clue that seeing her parents wasn't always the joyous occasion he had expected. "You...you're not happy about that?"

She lifted a shoulder. "I love them like anything. Lately, though, they've been way too overprotective."

"Thinking you're made of glass?"

"Yeah. Plus, they're disappointed in me."

"Why?" He couldn't imagine anyone less disappointing than Kelly.

"They want grandkids," she explained. "When my engagement ended, their chance for that ended, too."

"Wow." Alec was gobsmacked. The threads of this spider web were getting more and more tangled. They *had* a granddaughter; they just didn't know it.

She nodded, then sucked in a big breath and

blew it out in a sigh. "They're great. It'll be nice to see them."

From her tone, it was obvious she wasn't in the mood for a family visit.

Inside, the kitchen was warm and smelled like something delicious. Eldora bustled over to help with coats and packages.

"Hi, sweetie!" Kelly's mother knelt beside Zinnia, helping her unzip her coat. "Did you get a new dress?"

Zinnia nodded, leaning against Alec's leg.

"You can show us after lunch," Eldora said. "I made chili and cornbread."

"Chili!" Zinnia cried out, and threw her arms around Eldora's knees, her momentary shyness forgotten.

If Alec hadn't happened to look around the room right then, he might not have noticed the expressions on Kelly's and her mother's faces.

Longing.

They were both looking at Zinnia, and they were both full of longing. For what?

From the looks of things, a child. Or a grandchild.

Alec closed his eyes for the briefest moment. Zinnia needed family. *Alec* needed family.

And Mrs. Walsh needed a granddaughter. It just might mean everything to the woman, knowing that through Zinnia, a part of Chelsea lived on.

Fortunately, being the father of a young child offered few opportunities to worry about oneself or even think. Lunch went by in a blur of good food, toddler messiness and pleasant conversation. As long as Alec didn't focus on Kelly, he was fine.

The really amazing thing about Kelly was that she was fine, too, to all appearances. She obviously didn't want to cause any concern to anyone, including him. She talked and joked and helped her parents and Eldora connect with him and Zinnia. She hurried to get everyone drink refills and seconds.

Pokey stuck close to Zinnia, neatly grabbing every crumb she dropped.

Once the meal was over, Kelly went upstairs with Zinnia to help her change into her dress, which she insisted she wanted to model. Mrs. Walsh and Eldora shooed the "menfolk" out of the kitchen so they could do the dishes and chat.

"Just as well," Kelly's father said. "Wanted to talk with you."

Uh-oh. Alec followed the man into the front room, and they stood looking out the window at the snow.

The older man cleared his throat. "I don't want her hurt."

"Kelly?" Alec shook his head quickly. "I don't, either."

"She's been treated badly by a couple of losers."

Was Mr. Walsh calling him a loser, like the idiotic fiancé who'd dumped Kelly and taken up with Tonya? "I heard about that. Jerks."

Mr. Walsh looked at him expectantly.

Alec didn't want to make a vow he couldn't keep. "Look, I have feelings for her. But I'm aware it won't work and so I'm keeping my distance."

"Are you?"

Alec rubbed a hand over his jaw. This man was shrewd. "Trying to."

"Keep trying." Mr. Walsh clapped Alec on the back. "I like you, son. You didn't have it easy growing up. Now you've made something of yourself. Just don't know if you're ready to give my baby what she needs."

"Understood."

A light snow had started, and they stood watching it fall for a few more minutes.

Then they went back into the kitchen. They sat at the table and Eldora poured coffee, waving away the offer of help.

Zinnia came rushing into the kitchen in her dress. She stopped and twirled.

Alec's breath caught. She was so beautiful,

so sweet. He had to do everything he could for her. Had to keep her safe. Had to help her grow up strong.

He noticed a strange silence and glanced around the table.

"Oh, my," Eldora said finally.

Mr. and Mrs. Walsh were silent.

"I look pretty!" Zinnia cried.

"Yes, honey, you do," Alec said. He wasn't sure what was going on with the other adults.

"Very pretty," Kelly chimed in quickly. She looked confused, too.

"Oh, my, my, my," Eldora repeated. She sounded sad.

Mr. Walsh leaned closer to Mrs. Walsh and rubbed her arm. At which point Alec realized Mrs. Walsh had tears rolling down her face.

He looked at Eldora. "What's wrong?"

Eldora's smile was pensive. "She looks just like Kelly's sister, Chelsea, did in her pageant days."

Sweat broke out on Alec's forehead and neck. He could barely school his face. Fortunately, nobody was looking at him. They were all staring at Zinnia.

Was this the moment everything was going to come out?

If they guessed the truth about who Zinnia's mother was, it could be for the best. He wouldn't have to go back on his word to Chelsea. And Zinnia would get this, all these warm people loving her.

Of course, everyone would be angry at Alec for keeping the secret. But if it were better for Zinnia…

The little girl climbed into Mrs. Walsh's lap and touched her face. "You not like my dress?"

Mrs. Walsh laughed a little, grabbed a napkin and wiped her face. "I love it," she croaked out.

"You look just like someone we loved very much," Mr. Walsh said. His voice was a little thick, too.

Zinnia wrapped her little arms around Mrs. Walsh. "Feel better," she said. "Don't be sad."

Alec's chest swelled with love. No matter what happened, Zinnia would be amazing. Somehow amid the chaos of her early life, she'd grown a huge heart.

Eldora straightened and slapped her hands lightly on her thighs. "Well, Zinnia, you look so pretty. And you're a sweet, kind girl, too."

Mr. Walsh reached out and touched the red-and-pink ribbon in Zinnia's hair. "I like your bow," he said.

Kelly looked at Alec and lifted her eyebrows, her hands in a palms-up gesture. Almost like she was apologizing. She opened a box of her homemade cookies and put them on the table. "A little dessert, everyone."

People reached for cookies and Zinnia slid off Mrs. Walsh's lap and knelt beside Pokey. Was this moment really going to pass without anyone realizing the truth?

He blew out a sigh. He wasn't sure, anymore, what to hope for.

Chapter Nine

Late Wednesday afternoon, as the sun turned the sky orange and pink behind bare, spidery tree branches, Kelly studied the little house she and Alec had just pulled up to. The colorful lights that lined the eaves and decorated the bushes couldn't disguise how tiny it was. "Are you sure it's okay to bring Pokey in? Your brother has two kids, right? And another on the way?"

She wouldn't mind getting out of this social engagement. It would be nice to drop Alec and Zinnia off and drive his car home. They'd just done a library visit, which had meant spending three hours together, and her nerves were stretched thin.

She and Alec were getting along fine. They were acting like cordial friends. They'd worked together well at the library visit.

But always, just beneath the surface, was the memory of their kiss. Whenever she thought of it, she melted.

For about two seconds. And then she remembered how decisively he'd backed away.

She still felt drawn to him, but it was clear he didn't share the feeling.

She'd thought the breakup with Danny had been difficult. Now she suspected that her pain had mostly come from embarrassment. She'd started getting over him right away, and at this point she felt more relief than sadness about the loss of their planned marriage.

She and Alec hadn't been in a real relationship. They were just friends who'd kissed one evening. She couldn't let it go, though. Couldn't stop remembering how gentle he'd been and how wonderful his arms had felt around her. Being with him while pretending not to care was shockingly painful.

"It'll be a mob scene for sure," Alec said cheerfully, gesturing for her to go ahead of him on the walkway to the front door. He was holding Zinnia's hand. "But the kids will enjoy Pokey."

Still, she hesitated. "Are you sure a box of cookies is enough to bring?"

He looked at her sharply, ignoring the way Zinnia was tugging at his hand. "What's wrong?"

What to tell him? She couldn't exactly say

she kept thinking about their kiss. "I just don't want them to think we're a couple."

He frowned. "I told Cameron we aren't, but whether Jodi listens is a whole other thing." He put an arm around her shoulders for the briefest second, squeezed, and let go, leaving her breathless. "I'm sorry to make you uncomfortable. You don't have to come. I can take you home."

The front door opened, and a child's voice shouted, "They're here! They have a dog! And Zinnia!" His words were accompanied by a high-pitched yipping sound.

Zinnia pulled away from Alec and ran to the front door. Pokey strained a little at the leash.

"I'm serious," he said. "I can take you home." His eyes were warm, concerned.

When two eager young boys spilled out of the house, she shook her head. "I'm fine. It's fine. It'll be fun."

"You're sure?" He studied her face like he really saw her, really cared.

How could a heart feel warm and ache at the same time? "I'm sure. Let's go."

Inside the house, happy chaos reigned. A live Christmas tree dominated the small living room. The two boys she'd met while shopping for Zinnia's dress, probably three and six years old, jumped on the couch in exuberant energy. A small white mop of a dog observed the proceedings from the kitchen doorway, head cocked. That must be the emotional support dog Alec had told her about. Cameron greeted them both, clasping one of Alec's hands and one of Kelly's.

The air was fragrant with evergreen and something delicious from the kitchen. Five stockings hung along the mantel—one must be for the pup—and a half-completed kids' puzzle featuring Santa Claus covered the coffee table.

A lump lodged itself in Kelly's throat. This was how she'd do Christmas if she had kids. Festive, not fancy.

Jodi came out of the kitchen, a "Cute and Can Cook" apron over her sweatshirt and jeans. "Welcome, come in, get warm," she said, kneeling to give Zinnia a hug. "Hi, sweetie, we're so glad you're here. Boys, stop running around and take everyone's coats to the bedroom."

The boys slowed, but didn't stop until Cam added, "Boys, do what Mom said. Now."

"Okay, Mama," the younger boy said cheerfully, and started helping Zinnia out of her coat.

"I can take yours," the older boy said to Kelly.

Alec had told Kelly that the two boys were Cam's by his first wife. Apparently, she had abandoned the family and shown no interest in raising the boys to adulthood. Jodi had started out as a temporary nanny, but after she and Cam married, she'd adopted the boys. It was clear they now saw her as their mother.

Within another couple of minutes, Kelly and Alec were seated on the couch with glasses of warm cider in front of them. The boys had settled down on the floor with Zinnia. Everyone was introduced. Pokey stood patiently while Jodi's smaller dog sniffed her, giving an occasional yap.

A big box of toys sat beside the front door. "We're donating those to other kids who don't have much," the older boy explained when he saw Kelly looking at the box.

"That's very nice." It looked to Kelly like these kids might not have much, either; there certainly weren't a lot of toys strewn about, like she'd seen in some of her students' homes.

"It's to make room for our presents!" The younger boy hurried over to the tree, where five or six gifts were wrapped. "So far we all have two, but pretty soon, we might get more."

"Or *give* more," Jodi reminded them, her voice full of laughter. "I haven't seen anything down there with *my* name on it."

"We're making you—" the younger boy started eagerly.

"Shut up!" The older boy clapped a hand over his brother's mouth.

"Hector..." Cameron said warningly.

"We speak kindly in this house," Jodi added.

"Sorry," Hector said. "But he was gonna tell Mom what we're making!"

"Was *not*." The younger boy stuck out his lower lip.

"Seems to me," Jodi said, looking from Cam to Alec, "you gentlemen might like to help the kids with their puzzle. Or with whatever it is the boys are making for me. I'm going to finish up dinner." She looked at Kelly. "Want to come help?"

"Sure." Kelly wove through the kids and dogs and followed Jodi into a tiny, old-fashioned kitchen. "What can I do?"

"Make the salad, if you don't mind," Jodi said promptly. "Use that big bowl and whatever you can find in the produce drawer." She gestured toward an open laptop at a desk in the corner of the kitchen. "I'm a blogger, and I got too caught up in my work to prep for dinner like I should have."

They worked together companionably for a few minutes, talking about Jodi's blog, Kelly chopping vegetables while Jodi checked the status of a delicious-smelling meatloaf and stirred a big pan of chopped-up potatoes and onions.

"So," Jodi said, "how are things going with you and Alec?"

Kelly blinked. She barely knew Jodi and she

definitely didn't feel like confiding in her. So she went for a bland, safe answer. "We're doing great at the river house, thanks to my aunt, Eldora. She's been cooking us dinner most nights, and she watches Zinnia whenever Alec has errands to run."

Jodi didn't accept the deflection. "I meant the two of you together."

Why did people always think a single woman's love life was a good topic for discussion? Kelly hadn't come in asking Jodi about the state of her marriage, had she?

But Kelly had seen that the state of Jodi's marriage was excellent, just from the way she and Cam looked at each other. And she knew she was a little too touchy about people getting into her romantic business. So she decided to deliberately misunderstand the question she knew Jodi was really asking. "We visited a day care yesterday and did a library program today. Alec and Zinnia are a big help with showing the kids how to interact with Pokey."

"That's nice," Jodi persisted, "but what about romantically? Are you two dating?"

Nope, not getting out of this. Kelly shook her head. "No. I'm very content being single, and Alec—"

The other woman put a hand over her mouth. "I'm sorry. Cam really thinks you two would be great together, and now that I've met you, I think so, too. But I forgot that you just had a broken engagement."

"Wait, you know about that?" Kelly blew out a breath. "Everyone in Holiday Point has heard the story, but I didn't think the news would travel out of town."

Jodi chuckled. "Honey, we're starving for news out here. Our little country store is gossip central. Plus, Danny's the youth pastor at our church."

Of course. "If you know what happened," Kelly said, "I'm sure you can understand why I'm focusing on building an independent life."

Jodi pointed a spatula at her. "I do understand," she said, "probably more than you realize. I wanted to do that, too, although mine was due to some mental health issues."

Kelly blinked. "Oh, wow."

"Sorry." Jodi smiled, her expression rueful. "I used to be really closed about stuff, but since moving here and marrying Cam, I seem to have lost my filter."

"That's okay," Kelly said faintly. She wasn't used to this level of sharing from a near-stranger. Not that she minded. Her best friend was Olivia, and Olivia knew everything about her, but aside from that, she kept her cards close to her chest.

Which wasn't necessarily the road to happiness.

"Just don't give up on love," Jodi said. "Maybe Alec needs you, just like Cameron needs me."

Kelly shook her head. "I don't think Alec needs me, particularly."

Jodi waved a hand toward the living room. "They didn't have this kind of life, growing up. They didn't have family dinners or Christmas decorations or friends visiting. They don't quite know how to do it, but they really, really crave it."

Just then, the sound of Alec's laughter boomed out, and Kelly realized she hadn't heard it before. Not a loud, uninhibited laugh, at least. It was a good sound.

It made her think. Of course, she knew about Alec and Cam's family. They were notorious. She'd never stopped to think about what that had meant for Alec's upbringing, though. Hadn't put it all together.

"Plus," Jodi said, "the two of you light up when you're around each other. It's nice to see."

Kelly's chest warmed and her heart gave an extra beat. "We *do*?"

"You do." Noise from the other room had been growing, and now it reached a crescendo. "Now, let's get dinner on the table before this whole house erupts like a Christmas volcano."

As Kelly carried food and helped serve the

kids, Jodi's words kept coming back to her. Two statements in particular. "The two of you light up when you're around each other" and "Alec needs you."

Was it true? Was there maybe a chance for her and Alec to have something like what Jodi and Cameron shared?

After dinner, they all sat in the living room watching a movie. The adults claimed the couch while the kids and dogs lounged on the floor.

Alec had intended to leave right after dinner, but Kelly no longer seemed in a hurry to go. She laughed at the comedy on TV and chatted with Jodi and Cameron. She seemed to be enjoying herself.

He and Kelly sat side by side, and Alec desperately wanted to put his arm around Kelly the way Cameron was cuddling up with Jodi. But he restrained himself.

Cameron had taken him aside and asked him whether he'd told Kelly the truth about Zinnia. Then he'd scolded Alec for keeping such a secret from a woman who didn't deserve deception.

They'd talked a little about the obligation Alec had to Chelsea, his promise to her, the reasons she didn't want her identity as Zinnia's mother known. "It's not like you're any great shakes in the reputation department," Cam had told him bluntly. "There are plenty of people who judge our family harshly. Does that mean we shouldn't parent kids? Because I've got news for you: it's too late."

Alec had stuck to his plan and his promise, but after a lot of discussion, he'd agreed with Cameron that talking to the pastor about the situation would be a good idea. He'd promised to do so after Christmas.

The kids started dozing off, all clustered on the floor in front of the tree. When the movie ended, the four adults turned down the volume and chatted quietly. Eventually, Jodi and Cam went into the kitchen.

"Are you glad you came?" Alec asked Kelly. She hadn't scooted away from him on the couch, for which he was glad.

"It's been fun." She looked at the kids and smiled. "Your brother and Jodi are nice." She let out a wistful sigh.

Alec could have done the same. He felt wistful, too, thinking how much he'd enjoyed this evening and how much he'd like to have another like it.

And he could, for sure, if he and Zinnia stayed in Holiday Point. He and Zinnia could visit his brother often. Zinnia could have a real relationship with her cousins, and Alec and

Cameron could spend time together, raise their kids together, deal with their parents together.

What he couldn't do was bring Kelly along all the time, not if he wasn't in a relationship with her.

He needed to stop thinking about what couldn't happen. He found a holiday music station on the TV, and they chatted about their favorite Christmas songs. Kelly shared some of her family's holiday traditions: going caroling with another family, making advent calendars, eating lasagna on Christmas Eve. "It sounds nice," he said.

"It was." She paused. "Jodi said you and Cameron didn't have too many traditions growing up."

"Unless you count our parents drinking too much and getting into fights," he said mildly. "That was a given, every holiday."

"Did you kids get presents?" she asked.

He shrugged. "We did, sometimes, but they mostly came from charity groups. You know, the ones that have a tag that says 'Boy, Age 10' on it."

"Oh, that's bad." Her brow crinkled. "They should have at least taken the tag off!"

"Seriously, how hard would that be?" He smiled and shook his head. "Hey, we were grateful for the gifts."

After they'd talked a while longer and Jodi

and Cameron didn't come back, Alec went to look for them in the kitchen. They weren't there. And then his phone buzzed. His brother.

Sorry not to say goodbye. Don't wake up the kids when you go. Thanks, bro.

He went back out to the living room. "I think Cameron and Jodi are seizing the chance for some alone time," he said. "Let's try to slip out without waking up the kids."

"Oh!" Kelly blushed as understanding awakened in her eyes.

Alec found it sweet. In some ways, Kelly was naïve, certainly more so than he was. But he wished he could regain some of that naiveté. It was part of what made her seem surprised and delighted by the world so much of the time, which in turn was what made her so good with kids. She had a lot in common with them.

She roused Pokey gently, and he picked up Zinnia. Cameron's two boys lay on the floor beneath the tree, the little white dog curled up between them. On an impulse, Alec snapped a couple of pictures. Kelly found an afghan on the back of the sofa and tucked it around the boys and dog. Then they slipped out the front door.

The night was clear and cold. Stars shone overhead, and their breath made clouds in the air as they walked to the car. Snow and ice crackled under their feet, and the scent of the pines that lined one side of Cameron's driveway wafted toward them.

When he eased Zinnia into her car seat, she let out a few sleepy words and then fell instantly back to sleep. Pokey jumped in the car beside her and lay down.

"Pokey's tired, too," Kelly said, rubbing the dog's ears before closing the door gently on the two sleepyheads.

They drove in companionable silence for a while, and then Kelly spoke. "Did you and your brother have a good talk?"

"Yeah, we did." Actually, it had been a little uncomfortable when Cameron had pressed him to reveal the truth about Zinnia to Kelly and her family. But Alec knew Cameron had his and Zinnia's best interests at heart. He intended to take Cam's advice and talk about the situation with his new pastor after the holidays.

Of course, he didn't want to describe that part of the conversation to Kelly. "He told me our parents are having a party on the twenty-third," he said instead. "They want me to come and bring Zinnia."

"What would that be like?"

"Not good. I'd never ask you to go."

"Of course." He glanced over and saw that she was looking straight ahead. Not smiling.

He reviewed what he'd said. "Not because I

don't want to be with you, but because it's not the best environment." He paused. "They're my parents, and I need to see them sometime. I had coffee with Mom the other day, but I haven't seen Dad yet."

"Is he the difficult one?" she asked quietly.

"He is. Well, they both are, to tell you the truth. I might stop by for a little while."

She looked over at him. "I think you should. They're your parents."

"Apparently Cameron is going to make an appearance. I don't know if Jodi and the kids are coming or not. I for sure don't want to expose Zinnia to a party at their house, not yet."

"I can watch Zinnia if you don't want to take her," she offered.

Kelly was so sweet, always quick to make an offer to help. "I can't ask you to do that. I'm sure you'll have other plans. It's a Saturday night, right before Christmas."

She shrugged. "I'm okay with staying home."

That seemed strange. He'd have pictured her as the type who fielded a lot of invitations. "So what did you and Jodi talk about?"

She laughed a little. "How the two of us, you and me, should get together. Of course."

Alec's heart skipped a beat. It shouldn't, since there was no way he could get involved with Kelly, who had no idea of the secret he was carrying. "Jodi's relentless. Won't take no for an answer."

Kelly was quiet. He'd started to understand her silences, her emotions, and he looked over. Had he hurt her? He reached over and squeezed her hand. "If there was any way to make it work between us, I would want to try."

She pulled her hand away. "You don't have to say that."

Obviously, she didn't believe him. He pulled into the river house's driveway, parked, and turned off the car. As she started to open the door, he put a hand on her arm. "Hey," he said. "I mean that. I'd want us to explore this—" he gestured from himself to her and back again "—if there was a way it could work."

She studied his face. There were questions in her eyes, questions he couldn't answer. Still, he wanted her to believe him. He reached out and traced the side of her face with his finger. "You're a beautiful person," he said.

Her eyes narrowed for a moment and then she pulled away and got out of the car. "Come on, Pokey," she said as she opened the back door.

Then she went into the house without another word to him. Leaving him to consider that he must have *really* hurt her feelings.

But that was probably for the best, because there *wasn't* any way they could get together.

Chapter Ten

The day after the wonderful, intense visit to Alec's brother's house, Kelly was grateful to escape with her great-aunt. She and Eldora were visiting the senior community where Eldora had been living prior to her escape to the river house.

Kelly's mixed feelings about Alec were troublesome enough. Although Kelly wanted, sincerely, to be a strong single woman, the presence of Alec and Zinnia kept tugging her back in the direction of family and connection.

Every time Zinnia came into the room, Kelly wanted to pick up the little girl and hug her. And every time she saw Alec, Kelly's heart seemed to double its rate. Because she wouldn't mind hugging *him*, either.

What made it more difficult was that Alec was sending mixed messages. One minute, he was telling her he didn't want to bring her to his family party. The next, he was touching her face with a tenderness that burned like fire.

It was way too confusing. Time to focus on other people, not on herself.

The Penn Senior Villas looked like any other apartment building in the area, except that it adjoined a nursing home. Four stories, brick, with wrought-iron railings around the units that had balconies. It was too cold for anyone to be outside, but once they entered, receiving friendly greetings from most of the clusters of residents and staff in the lobby, the place's liveliness became apparent. This *wasn't* just any apartment building. There was a real sense of community here.

Eldora put a hand on Kelly's arm. "Thanks for doing this with me," she said. "I would really like to just drop these gifts off and go, but I should probably stay and visit for a little while."

"I'm glad to do it," Kelly said. "Pokey specializes in kids, but I'd like to give her more practice with seniors as well. Every type of group has special concerns and it's good for her to get used to variety."

"Plenty of walkers and oxygen tanks here," Eldora said, grimacing.

Kelly looked at her aunt. "Is that what you don't like about living here?"

Eldora sighed. "Part of it. It's wrong of me, but I don't like the reminder of what's probably in my future."

Compassion filled Kelly's heart. "I can't imagine what that must be like," she said honestly. "Although I guess I will one day. I do know that you're strong and healthy and have a lot of life in front of you."

"Thank you for that, dear. I should be kinder and more accepting. I just hate how everyone discusses their ailments!"

Kelly smiled and squeezed her shoulder. "Then I'm glad you could escape and spend the holidays with me."

The elevator pinged and they rode up to the third-floor activity room. "Howdy, Miss Eldora," said one man instantly, coming over. A couple of women waved from the table where they were playing cards. One of the women was using a wheelchair, and as they walked into the room, another man entered the recreation area, leaning on a rolling walker.

Kelly held Pokey back, wanting her to get used to the equipment. It had been part of her training to learn to be around crutches and walkers and wheelchairs, but that had been almost a year ago. Kelly didn't want Pokey to get spooked and leap back from one of the residents, possibly hurting their feelings.

The man with the walker made his way over to them, though, and Pokey's tail wagged. She was so good at being a therapy dog and she loved giving and getting attention.

The man reached out for Pokey, and she bent her head to be petted, tail still wagging.

"Aren't you a good dog!" the man said. "What kind is she, a whippet?"

"Greyhound," Kelly said. "She was a former racer, but now she really enjoys just lying around."

As if to prove the point, Pokey lay down with a thump, revealing her belly for a rub.

"Ah, sweet dog. Sure wish I could get down there to pet her, but my joint pain is kicking up something awful today."

Kelly glanced at Eldora, who gave her a wry smile. Kelly could imagine that the discussion of ailments could get irritating at times.

Another woman who'd been reading came over and knelt beside Pokey, rubbing her belly. "Therapy dog, eh?" she said, reading the vest Kelly had put on Pokey for the occasion. "Plenty of work for you here. We could all use some therapy."

"Especially you," the man with the walker joked.

"I'm not the only one, Harold Johnson." The woman stood up and raised an eyebrow at him.

They spent about fifteen minutes in the recreation room, and Pokey performed like a champ, visiting everyone, keeping a comfortable distance from those who held back. It was always hard, but important, to remember that not everyone loved dogs. However, Pokey was good at winning most people over.

Eldora visited with several people in the room and also delivered gifts to several of the staff and residents. Kelly was glad to see that she seemed to be getting over her resistance to spending time here. Having friends and a sense of community was as important for Eldora as for anyone else, now that she'd moved back from the big city.

"Anyone in particular you want to visit?" Kelly asked her.

"Yes. My childhood best friend, Molly Kircher."

"That's not Miss Kircher who taught piano, is it? And goes to our church?"

"It is."

Kelly was excited for the chance to visit the woman who'd taught piano to her and most of the other musical kids in Holiday Point. When they got to her apartment, Eldora knocked, then called out, "I know you're in there, Molly. I brought a guest. Two of them, really." She turned to Kelly. "It may take her awhile. She has severe arthritis."

Slow footsteps sounded, then the door opened and a white-haired woman appeared behind it. She used a cane and was bent so far over that it seemed an effort for her to look up and greet them. When she did, though, her face crinkled into a smile. "Kelly Walsh!" she said. "And who is this with you?"

"This is Pokey," Kelly said. "She's a therapy dog."

"How wonderful! I miss having a dog. Thank you for bringing yours to share with us, dear."

"Well, stop gushing and invite us in," Eldora said.

Miss Kircher shook her head, still smiling. "Is Eldora as bossy to you as she is to me?" she asked. Then she turned and led the way to a small living room. She clicked off the television. "What can I get you ladies to drink?"

Kelly started to wave away the offer, not wanting to put Miss Kircher to any trouble. But Eldora caught her eye and gave a minuscule shake of her head.

"I'll have a glass of iced tea," Eldora said, "if you have any. Otherwise, water."

"Same for me," Kelly said. Then, it was hard to restrain herself from helping the older woman. But she understood from Eldora's silent communication that she shouldn't treat Miss Kircher differently from any other friend.

Miss Kircher poured three glasses of iced tea. "I'm going to ask you to carry your own drinks into the living room," she said, and Kelly stood quickly, glad for the chance to offer at least a little help.

As soon as they'd all sat down, Pokey went to Miss Kircher and leaned against her chair. Miss Kircher rubbed Pokey's head. "What a sweetheart you are," she said. "You can come visit me anytime. And you too, of course," she said, looking up at Kelly with laughter in her eyes. "You were one of my most dedicated students."

"Dedicated if not talented," Kelly said. She'd practiced dutifully, but she'd realized that she was better at listening to music than making it. "You were an extremely patient teacher."

"Oh, I loved the kids, especially the ones who worked hard, like you," the older woman said. Then her expression sharpened. "I was invited to your wedding. I'm so sorry about what happened."

Kelly blew out a sigh and then, looking inside herself, she realized she didn't mind the comment as much as she would have even a couple of weeks ago. "Thank you," she said. "I'm fine, though."

"That young man wasn't a good match for you," Miss Kircher said decisively.

"You know," Kelly said, "I think you may be right."

Pokey came over and nosed Kelly's hand, then. Either begging for a dog biscuit or offering comfort, maybe a little of both. Kelly reached into her treat bag and made Pokey sit and shake hands before rewarding her with a tiny dog cookie.

"I heard another rumor," Miss Kircher said, "about Alec Wilkins. Heard he was your new boyfriend, in fact."

Kelly couldn't help blushing. "Nothing to that," she said.

"They *are* living together," Eldora said, then waved a hand at Kelly's protest. "Kidding. They're sharing the river house that belongs to the Baldwins, and I'm there too, chaperoning."

"You?" Miss Kircher laughed. "You're probably the one in need of a chaperone. This one got in a fair amount of trouble when we were teenagers," she added to Kelly.

That led the two of them into some entertaining reminiscences that lasted until Kelly and Eldora had to leave. As they walked out, Kelly said, "I want to be single and happy and independent, like the two of you."

Eldora stopped her with a hand on her arm. "Don't model yourself on me. You have love right in front of you, and you should embrace it."

"What do you mean?" Kelly was pretty sure she knew what Eldora meant, but her aunt was way off base.

"There's a reason you and Alec needed a chaperone," her aunt teased. "And it's not just public opinion."

"We don't," Kelly protested. "Alec doesn't care for me that way."

"Are you sure about that?" Eldora asked. "I've seen the man looking at you."

That wasn't what Kelly wanted to hear. She was having enough trouble with her own feelings. "I need support in being single," she said, "not encouragement to get together with someone. Besides, you're happy with your life, aren't you?"

"I am," Eldora said, "but there are challenges in any state of life, being single among them." They headed out to the car, slowly. "The best thing to do is to follow the Lord's leading. If He wants you to be single, He'll help you make that happen."

"Like He did when Danny broke up with me," Kelly said.

"Yes. He'll also steer you away from the wrong person." She smiled at Kelly. "It's hard, but you need to just rest in the Lord and follow His leading."

Kelly knew that was absolutely true. She just wasn't quite sure of how to do it.

On Friday night, Alec took Zinnia to Holiday Point's annual dog parade. Alone. Not with Kelly and Pokey, who were an integral part of the event.

He'd wanted to drive her there, wanted to hang out with her beforehand, but he forced himself to keep his distance. He *had* to back off from her or he'd find himself doing more inappropriate things like he'd started to do in the car the other night.

They walked slowly along the main street of town, Zinnia in her rarely used stroller, since she seemed tired. It was a warmer evening, in the forties, and it seemed like the entire population of Holiday Point was taking advantage of the opportunity to get out and enjoy a family event. The parade took place on the little stretch of path that led to the park.

Alec hadn't realized there were that many dogs in the area. Hounds and Chihuahuas dressed up in Christmas costumes, some quite ornate. Three identical pugs wore green elf costumes, a tall, slender poodle was Mrs. Claus, and an enormous Great Dane was dressed to look like the Grinch. One large brown dog was dressed as a Christmas package, with wrapping paper and a bow around its middle. Pokey was a hit in her red Christmas sweater. A table of townspeople served as judges, but the competition was good natured; and the main point seemed to be for people to donate money to help a local dog rescue.

After the parade, most people made their way to the spot where two rivers came together, forming the point of the park. There, near the giant Christmas tree, a group of carolers sang, and several stands were set up with food: roasted nuts and popcorn and hot chocolate. Zinnia climbed out of her stroller, excited.

He was standing in line for some hot chocolate, Zinnia hopping beside him, when he heard Kelly's name from the women in front of him. He tuned in immediately.

"Did you hear that Danny's going to propose to Tonya tonight?" one of the women asked the others.

"In front of everyone?" the other woman said. "How can he do that to Kelly?"

"I wonder if she gave him back the ring."

"And if he'll use the same one for Tonya," the other woman said, shaking her head. "The whole thing is tacky. I'm guessing Tonya orchestrated it."

Alec veered out of the line immediately, ignoring Zinnia's protests, then fumbled in the stroller storage for a snack to placate her.

He had to find Kelly and warn her. Hopefully, get her away from here.

Alec wasn't a violent man, but he felt the urge to punch Danny.

Finally, he spotted Kelly. She was in the thick of the crowd, talking to a man and a woman. She wore a Santa hat to match Pokey's Christmas outfit.

"Here we go." The man gestured toward the Christmas tree, a disgusted expression on his face.

Alec saw immediately what they were looking at: Tonya and Danny, just a short distance away and clearly visible. Tonya seemed to be scanning the crowd. Danny looked…not exactly happy.

Kelly's wrinkled brow suggested she knew exactly what was about to happen. Alec approached and put a hand on her arm. "Hey. Let's get you out of here," he said quietly.

"I'm fine," Kelly said. "I don't need to run away."

There were murmurs in the crowd as the carolers were shushed and someone turned on a loud recording of John Legend's "All of Me."

People had formed a loose circle around Tonya and Danny, just like kids used to do when there was a fight after school. Alec had participated in a few of those. He felt like using some of that aggression against the smirking couple right now. What on earth were they thinking?

Danny sank to his knees. Tonya gestured to someone, maybe several someones, filming the event with their phones.

Kelly had her hand on Pokey's head, but she didn't look distressed. More like bemused.

Her friend from the couple who'd been talking with her nudged Kelly. "He didn't do a public proposal for you, did he?"

She shook her head. "Nope. I wouldn't have wanted one. He proposed in my parents' living room."

Danny seemed to be doing some sort of speech. Then, he pulled a box from his pocket with a flourish and opened it.

Tonya looked inside and her smile faltered. "It's so small," she said. She wasn't speaking loudly, but she was one of those people whose voices carried. "I told you what I wanted."

"What an awful woman," Kelly's friend said.

People were murmuring, but quietly. Everyone seemed to want to see how Danny would respond.

"I'm a youth pastor," Danny said, his voice audible now in the silence. "I can't afford a great big ring." He looked around at the crowd as if seeking affirmation for that.

His eyes rested on Kelly.

She lifted her hands, palms up.

"If it's the same one he gave you," Kelly's friend said, "it *was* kind of small."

"That's not what's important," she said. "Or it wasn't. To me."

"Matches the size of his heart," Alec said disgustedly.

Several people nearby laughed.

Tonya now pulled Danny to his feet and embraced him. It wasn't clear whether she'd said yes or no, but she did seem to recognize that the crowd wasn't on her side.

More murmuring started up. The love song ended, and someone turned off the speaker, and the carolers started up again.

People were nudging each other and looking at Kelly. Alec checked her face to see if she was upset. "Are you okay?" he asked her. "What a jerk."

"I'm fine," she said, laughing a little and shaking her head. "I'm just so thankful to be out of that engagement. So thankful not to be Tonya."

"No matter the occasion, you could never be her." In his own mind, Alec pictured proposing to Kelly. How would he do it? Definitely not in front of a big crowd. Too risky, plus, he felt like such an intimate moment should be private.

He'd come to the parade intending to keep his

distance from Kelly, but instead, he was thinking about proposing to her. Great. Just great. Still, he wanted to make sure she was okay. Wanted to protect her from anyone who thought about saying something mean. "Do you want to walk around together?" he asked. "Since we're here?"

Chapter Eleven

Kelly walked alongside Alec, trying to process what had just happened.

Her former fiancé—the man she'd planned to marry until two months ago—had just proposed to another woman. In public.

It should have added to the sense of public humiliation she'd had, having to revoke all those wedding invitations. To the anger and frustration she'd felt talking to the vendors they'd booked, trying to be fair while recouping some of her investment.

Instead, she felt…lighter. It was as if a weight had lifted off her in the moment Danny had uttered his proposal with that sheepish expression on his face.

She'd felt sorry for him, pity rather than anger. And she'd felt zero regret. A man who would do what Danny had done, either from insensitivity or from being weak enough to be pushed into a proposal, was not a man she wanted to spend her life with.

Although the experience had been painful, getting dumped by Danny might be one of the best things that had ever happened to her.

She looked over at Alec. She wasn't sure what she felt for him. Attraction, confusion, fear of being hurt again. But one thing she knew for sure was that he'd never, ever do what Danny had just done. He was too strong of a person. He'd never let a woman manipulate him into an act he didn't believe in, and he'd never do something that inconsiderate or unkind.

She was going to pay attention to her feelings, and maybe, just maybe, give him a chance.

They were almost to the edge of the crowd when people started coming up to her.

A high school friend gripped her hand. "I can't believe he did that."

One of her fellow teachers hugged her. "Are you okay?"

Mrs. Cramer, who'd helped with Zinnia's dress, said, "They deserve each other."

Kelly tried to take the remarks in the spirit in which they'd been given. People were being kind. "I'm fine, really. Thanks," she said, over and over again.

She walked faster, eager to escape the crowd.

"Watch out, it's icy," Alec said. He crooked his arm and tucked hers into it.

Alec's muscles were impressive. She could feel them through his heavy coat. She found herself cuddling closer.

She loosened her grip and started to ease away when she saw raised eyebrows from a couple of her friends. But what did it matter, really? She was getting a major lesson in not caring what others thought.

So she shrugged and hugged his arm again.

Soon, the crowd thinned. Cold, fresh air soothed her flushed face. The sound of talk and laughter and music receded behind them.

They passed the church, its steeple illuminated by a floodlight. She drew in a breath and let it out in a sigh, her tight shoulders relaxing.

She was going to have to learn to rest in Jesus, like Aunt Eldora had said. What else could she do?

"Are you sure you feel okay about walking home?" Alec was looking at her, his brow wrinkled. "Cameron's here with his kids. I'm sure he'd run us to the river house."

"I'm really fine, but thanks." She should probably let go of his arm, but…not quite yet.

"What man would do that?" Alec was shaking his head. "I'm sorry it happened. You didn't deserve that."

"It'll be a story for the ages, in this town," she said. "I can't believe I'm not upset. Do you think I'm in shock?"

"Do you still have feelings for the man?"

"No. Which doesn't speak well for me. I agreed to marry him and we were going through with it until two months ago."

"Everyone makes mistakes in love. It's good you figured out the truth about that guy before marriage."

"Better late than never, I guess." She looked sideways at him. "Have *you* made mistakes in love?"

He stiffened. The question hung in the air.

Maybe she should retract it. Asking about past romantic history was touchy. But she couldn't help being curious, especially about Zinnia's mother. Did Alec consider his relationship with her to be a mistake?

Finally, he spoke. "I've definitely made mistakes. I feel grateful that God's used some of them for good."

"Like Zinnia?"

"Like Zinnia. She's the light of my life."

She squeezed his arm and he looked down at her. Their eyes met and held, and suddenly, Kelly felt breathless.

He smiled and shook his head, and they walked on. Kelly felt in accord with him, in a way she'd never felt with anyone in her life. Strange, when there was no commitment or agreement between them, when they weren't even dating. Was it just a really intense kind of friendship?

They walked in quiet togetherness, and when they finally approached the river house, he slowed and then turned to her. "I don't want this to end," he said.

Kelly didn't, either, but she was confused. She looked up at him. Was he going to kiss her again? Was she going to let him?

He put his hands on her shoulders, and Kelly's heart started to pound.

But instead of kissing her, he spoke. "There are reasons I can't and shouldn't move forward with this," he said, "but I'm working on them. Kelly, I'm coming to care for you more and more."

She stared at him, her breathing quickening. "I care for you, too, but I don't trust my feelings. I've made terrible choices in the past."

He inclined his head as if to agree. "I'd consider myself a bad choice, too." As she started to protest, he pulled her into a hug. "Kelly, Kelly, Kelly. I didn't expect this when I came home to Holiday Point."

Kelly hadn't expected it, either. They were closer than ever, and he said he cared for her. But what were the mysterious reasons he couldn't move forward?

* * *

On Saturday night, Alec pulled into the rutted gravel driveway of the house where he'd grown up. A floodlight illuminated the ramshackle front porch.

He parked among the other cars and trucks, five or six of them, and just sat.

Even a coating of snow couldn't conceal the sagging of the roof nor the tall, dry weeds in what passed for a garden in front of the house. How much longer could his parents live here before the place fell down around them?

He'd visited his mom here last week, during the day when his dad was away, so the rundown state of the property didn't surprise him. Now, lights were on inside and the sound of music and raucous voices poured out the front door. It took him back.

His parents had often thrown parties to celebrate the season. They'd had friends and a few distant relatives in. He remembered being excited as a little kid, knowing that there were— or at least might be—gifts under the tree and cousins to play with. As he'd grown older, he'd dreaded the parties, because Dad had often gotten angry-drunk and taken out his feelings on his four boys. Almost better were the times Dad was away. Those years, Mom would be morose and crying. But because of charity groups that looked after the families of prisoners, they were more likely to have presents under the tree.

Now, hearing the noise, seeing a couple of guys stumble outside, arguing and shoving at each other, he was glad he hadn't brought Kelly or Zinnia.

He was here to figure out how to deal with his family, as a step toward making a change. His feelings for Kelly had become overwhelming, and he hadn't known how to express them well. He'd been up and down, friendly and then abrupt with Kelly, and he knew he'd confused her.

He had to figure out a way to pursue a relationship with her if he could.

He checked his phone, but there was no reception out here. That figured. He got out of the car and walked toward the house, his boots crunching in the snow.

Inside, along with the shouts of greetings, more memories assailed him. The slightly musty smell of the house. Mom's favorite chair, covered with a floral slipcover. The kitchen table, topped with bowls and bags of chips and bottles of liquor. He set down the platter of cheeses and meats he'd picked up at the store.

His mother, an apron over her faded jeans and sweater, hurried over and wrapped her arms around him. "You came! My big son." Her words were slurred.

He hugged her back, love and frustration warring within him. Over her shoulder, he saw Fiscus in an armchair, a woman in his lap. Dad sat in a recliner, the TV remote in one hand and a glass of some amber-colored liquor in the other. Several other people Alec didn't know stood around, talking and laughing.

He let go of his mother, and she turned to speak with someone else. He caught sight of Cam, who lifted an eyebrow and grinned and shook his head, all at once. *Here we go again,* his expression seemed to say.

Alec walked over to his father, whom he hadn't seen on his earlier visit. White stubble on a weathered face, long, thinning hair… Dad was aging. A lot. But he managed to stand and shake Alec's hand.

"About time you showed up. How about a beer?" Without waiting for an answer, he pulled one out of the cooler beside his chair and handed it to Alec.

Alec hadn't had anything to drink in a long time, but alcohol might ease the tension of this gathering. His throat felt dry, and he started to open the bottle.

Apparently done socializing, Dad turned his attention back to the TV. Alec looked over at Cam, who stood talking to Mom now. Cam, he noticed, was drinking a soda.

Alec was relieved anew that he hadn't brought his daughter to this gathering. He'd been wavering, but she'd come down with a cold and Kelly had offered to stay home with her. It had seemed like a good solution at the time, and now, it seemed like a really good one. This wasn't an environment for kids.

He walked over to the refrigerator and set the unopened beer inside.

After making small talk with some of the other guests, Alec sat down beside Fiscus and the woman who was apparently his girlfriend. He searched his mind for something to talk about. His usual mode with Fiscus was bailing him out of trouble.

He settled for "Merry Christmas, bro."

"Same to you." Fiscus raised his glass and took a long drink. "This is Darlene. Darlene, my brother Alec."

"Hello," she said, smiling at him. She was still sitting in Fiscus's lap. "You're the soldier, right?"

"Was. Now I'm just a guy looking for a job."

That seemed to put Fiscus at ease. He fist-bumped Alec. "Same, man. Same."

"Any leads?"

Fiscus lifted a shoulder and took another drink. "Doing some carpentry."

"He's making me a corner cabinet for Christmas!" Darlene said.

"Nice." He remembered that Fiscus, who'd worked as a medic in the military, had always been good with his hands. They all were, really. Cam was a whiz with automotive stuff, and Alec enjoyed the trade he'd picked up in the military, repairing heavy equipment. Fiscus, he remembered, had been an artistic kid. At least until their father had beaten him for asking to go to art camp. Alec still didn't know if the beating had been because Dad didn't think art was manly, or because he didn't want to admit he couldn't afford the camp.

Alec should have spent more time getting to know his youngest brother and defending him from their father's fists. Instead, he'd been bent on escape.

Loud voices pulled him from his thoughts. Dad was yelling at Cam, and Mom was trying to quiet him down, and crying.

"Oh, boy," Alec said, and stood.

Fiscus rolled his eyes and poured himself another drink from the bottle beside him.

"I ain't seen those kids in half a year," Dad was saying. "You never bring them around. We're not good enough for you? You're breaking your mother's heart."

"You're invited over for New Year's Day," Cam said evenly.

"Yeah, no drinking allowed," Dad said, glowering.

"You're welcome to come, too," Cam said, turning to Alec.

"Thanks," Alec said. "Zinnia and I will be there."

"Yeah, who's this Zinnia? Never even met her." Dad lifted his hands. "Neither of you boys act like part of the family."

Their argument had penetrated the noise, and others were gathered around. Cam glanced at Alec. "About time for me to take off."

Dad grunted his disapproval.

"I'll head out, too," Alec said. He shook his father's hand and then turned away before Dad could start in on him. He hugged his mother. "Are you going to be okay with him?" he asked quietly.

"I'm fine." She clung a little. "He's mad at you, not me. But really, he's mad at himself."

Alec got his coat and, after making sure his father wasn't watching, pulled out a fifty-dollar bill and slipped it to his mother. He thought about telling her to spend it on something other than booze, but he didn't. Wouldn't do any good.

"Thanks, honey," she slurred. "Merry Christmas."

Outside, he walked with Cam toward the parked cars. Snow crunched under their feet, and overhead was a sky full of stars. Alec breathed in the cold air and relaxed his tight shoulders. "That went well," he joked.

Cam snorted. "Right." He shook his head. "Mom and Dad. They don't change."

"Maybe we shouldn't have gone," Alec said. "I don't know that it did any good."

"Yeah. I don't know, either." Cam reached his car and stopped, and Alec stopped beside him. "What I do know," Cam said, "is that what they do isn't our fault. Even if Dad tries to make us think it is."

"I guess," Alec said doubtfully.

"I mean," Cam went on, "is it Zinnia's fault that Chelsea went downhill?"

"Of course not!" The idea was ridiculous.

Cam looked at him steadily.

"Which means," Alec said, "that you're right. Mom and Dad's issues aren't our fault, either."

"Bingo." Cam whacked him gently on the arm and turned toward his car. "Want to stop over for a little while?"

Alec shook his head. "Thanks, but I need to do a couple of quick errands and then get home." Home to Zinnia and Kelly. Because if his parents' bad behavior wasn't his fault, then maybe he wasn't too flawed and messed up for a woman like Kelly.

Of course, before he could pursue the relationship he wanted with Kelly, he had to tell her the truth. Very, very soon.

Chapter Twelve

Kelly sat in the rocking chair in Alec and Zinnia's little suite of rooms, Zinnia crying quietly in her arms.

"It's okay, honey. You'll be okay." She brushed curls back from the child's flushed, sweaty face. "Just sleep. You'll feel better."

"Daddy," Zinnia said fretfully. "Want Daddy."

"Daddy will be here when you wake up. Shh." Kelly reached for her phone and found a lullaby soundtrack. The music played, soft and low, and Zinnia yawned.

Kelly did, too. She'd been trying to get Zinnia to sleep for the past hour. She hoped she could stay awake long enough for that to happen.

Who'd have thought Kelly would spend the Saturday night before Christmas caring for a sweet, sick baby?

It was to have been her wedding night.

She and Danny had planned a December twenty-third wedding, which probably hadn't been very practical, thinking of how busy people were at this time of year. But it was definitely romantic. An image of what the beautifully decorated church would have looked like, of her burgundy-clad bridesmaids, of the flowers she'd picked out, flashed through her mind.

When she thought about Danny, though, the bubble burst. A pretty, romantic wedding would have been nice—to the right man. Which Danny wasn't.

Zinnia was quieting down now, her little fussy cries further and further apart. "You're getting sleepy," Kelly crooned, hoping to make it so.

Then again, she didn't mind rocking the little girl as long as she needed it. Zinnia was a sweetheart, and Kelly felt fortunate to be in her life.

She even had some hope that she'd continue to be a part of Zinnia's life, but it was all dependent on Alec. He'd said something amazing: that he wanted to pursue this thing that was happening between them. But since last night when they'd walked home from the dog parade and he'd said he was working on his barriers, he'd been up and down. Close one minute and distant the next.

It was confusing. The discouragement she'd

felt when she and Danny had broken up warred with a bright sense of hope and excitement that kept bubbling up when she thought of Alec.

Maybe she was making better choices now. Maybe this could work.

Finally, Zinnia seemed to be sleeping. Her breathing was steady, although she was congested enough to make the occasional little snoring sound. Carefully, Kelly lifted her into her portable crib.

Kelly breathed a sigh of relief. And then Zinnia let out a particularly loud snort, woke herself up and wailed.

Kelly felt the child's forehead. Was it her imagination, or was she more feverish? Did she need medicine or to go to the doctor?

When Alec left, Zinnia had seemed just slightly congested. She was definitely getting worse. Wasn't she? Or was this just a twenty-four-hour bug that would be gone tomorrow?

Kelly sent a text to Alec, nothing alarming, just describing the symptoms, and then got a wet cloth to wipe Zinnia's face. She found an ear thermometer in the bathroom and took Zinnia's temperature. Still just slightly elevated.

There was no answer from Alec. She knew he'd been planning to go to a party at his parents' and then to pick up a few last-minute things for Zinnia's stocking, so it made sense that he wasn't answering. Her mother and Eldora, the two people she'd like to consult about a sick child, were probably busy now, too. Plus, neither one was the type to carry a phone around at all times.

She put on another round of lullabies and patted Zinnia's back. "Go to sleep, sweet girl," she crooned. Sleep was what would do the most good, Kelly was pretty sure.

She'd been around plenty of sick kids as a first-grade teacher, but then, her approach was to get them away from other kids and home to recuperate as quickly as possible. Being in charge of a younger kiddo was a different thing entirely.

She continued gently rubbing Zinnia's back with one hand while she searched "congested baby won't sleep" with the other. Okay, so a humidifier would be a good idea, but she doubted there was one in the house. Saline nose drops? How did you use those without freaking the little one out? Suddenly, Kelly felt like she knew nothing about baby care.

There was an emergency clinic in Uniontown, but would it be open on Saturday night? Very doubtful. It was the ER or nothing, and Zinnia didn't seem sick enough for the ER.

Maybe there was some baby cold medicine Alec used for her. She checked her phone again. No answer.

She went through the bedroom to the bathroom, hoping to find a baby syringe for the saline drops. If she could find that, she could google how to use it. Plus, if Alec had a syringe, it would mean Zinnia was at least a little accustomed to that treatment. That was probably the best option.

She sent Alec another text. Surely he'd check his messages, considering he didn't have Zinnia with him?

As she walked back across Alec's bedroom and into Zinnia's, she saw a stack of folders on his desk. The top one said "Zinnia—Health Records."

Hmm. That seemed relevant. Maybe there was an address of her new pediatrician, or even an emergency contact Kelly could call for advice.

She flipped through the paperwork, noting that a doctor had prescribed children's Tylenol. Good. Maybe there was some in the house somewhere, or maybe Alec could pick some up on the way home.

She straightened the papers in the folder and turned to go soothe Zinnia again when a small half-sheet of paper fell out of the stack.

Certificate of Birth.

Kelly smiled and picked it up. When she glanced over it, a familiar name jumped out at her.

In the "mother" box, Chelsea Walsh was listed.

Kelly's heart pounded so hard she felt like she might pass out. She let the piece of paper flutter to the ground.

It didn't seem possible, but there it was in black and white.

Zinnia was Chelsea's daughter.

Alec drove home from the big-box store, smiling about the little toys he'd picked up for Zinnia. Despite Kelly's assurances, he hated to be out so late. She'd texted him that Zinnia wasn't feeling well a couple of times, but of course, in his parents' place, the texts hadn't come through. He'd been too preoccupied to check his phone after the disturbing party, and then he'd gotten caught up in his last-minute purchases.

When he'd finally seen the texts and tried to call, there was no answer. That wasn't surprising; it was late. She must have turned her phone off and gone to bed, which meant Zinnia had gotten better.

He'd learned something from Olivia, whom he'd run into at the store: today was to have been Kelly's wedding day. No wonder she'd been fine with staying home with Zinnia, rather than going out to any parties.

He felt for her. The end of a relationship was always rough, not that he'd had many serious ones himself. For a sensitive woman like Kelly, to have the breakup happen so publicly must have been painful. He couldn't be sorry she wasn't marrying that jerk who'd proposed to Tonya in the park. What was the guy thinking?

Alec wanted to be the man who'd treat her better. She deserved it. And he was starting to think that maybe, just maybe, he could be that man.

Being at his parents' house and talking to Cam had made him realize that he wasn't to blame for the childhood he'd had or for his family's reputation. He hadn't been perfect, still wasn't, but he and Cam had moved beyond the family issues. It wasn't their fault that their parents and brother still caused problems in the community. He wanted to try to help his parents, and Fiscus too, but he was through blaming himself for their choices.

And if he wasn't to blame for the past, then he could be optimistic about the future.

He just had to come clean about Zinnia's origins, to Kelly and her family.

Now wasn't the time. But after the holidays, he was going to talk to the pastor and figure out how to deal with his promise to Chelsea. Hopefully, he'd figure out a way to tell the truth to Kelly and her parents. And then they'd see about whether to tell the rest of the community. It was possible that Chelsea had been wrong in her assumption that Zinnia would be treated badly because of Chelsea's mistakes. He was pretty sure that most people in the community would realize that Zinnia was an innocent child, not a carbon copy of her mother.

He parked and walked toward the house, pausing halfway in awe of the beauty of his surroundings. The snow had veiled everything in white, and the sky seemed to hold a million stars. Looking down toward the river, he saw bushes and small trees coated with ice, sparkling in the moonlight.

He shot up a prayer of thanks for the beauty and the blessings in his life. And then he walked in the door.

He saw Kelly immediately. She was sitting on the stairs holding something in her hand. There was a box of tissues beside her, and she'd obviously been crying.

His heart seemed to reach out of his chest, feeling her pain as his own. He hurried toward her. "I heard this was to have been your wedding day. I'm sorry." He held out a hand to her. "Come sit on the couch and I'll get you something to drink."

She ignored his hand, but she did stand. "It's not that."

There was something in her face, her voice. Anger?

She held out the piece of paper, and he took it and glanced at it, figuring it was related to the canceled wedding.

And then he saw the words "birth certificate," and his world crashed around him.

He took a step back and opened his mouth to speak, but he couldn't find words.

"Why didn't you tell me," she asked, her voice even, "that Zinnia is Chelsea's child?"

So it was out. The secret was out. And looking at Kelly's wrecked face, he realized just how wrong he'd been to hide the truth.

He felt like a kid who'd been caught tormenting a puppy or kitten. What a complete jerk he'd been to think it was okay to keep this secret. He should have arrived in town and called a meeting of Kelly and her parents immediately, and explained the situation.

It was just that he'd promised not to do that, and he had always prided himself on keeping his word. That was how he showed the world that he wasn't like his parents, that he was better.

Only he wasn't better.

He looked at the pink Christmas tree in the corner. He'd bought it for Zinnia to make her happy, but he hadn't done the real, big thing that could make her happy: he hadn't given her the aunt and grandparents who were rightfully hers. A pink Christmas tree couldn't begin to make up for what he'd done wrong.

Kelly's hands were on her hips, her expression full of righteous anger. "Why didn't you tell me? Tell *us*?"

There was no explanation that would solve this, but still, for Zinnia's sake, he tried. "Chelsea made me promise—"

"You've been here all this time," Kelly interrupted. "You've talked about Chelsea. We sat in this very room and talked about her. And yet you lied."

He'd been careful not to lie, but he'd been deceptive enough that keeping the letter of the law didn't matter. "I didn't feel I could break my promise to your sister."

She looked at him like he was something stuck on the bottom of her shoe. That made him realize she normally looked at him with kindness and good feelings. With caring. It made him see they might have had a chance together.

Not now, though. Through his own actions, that chance was as gone as the planned Christmas wedding that had been canceled.

"How long were you in a relationship with her?" Kelly demanded. "Was it the whole time, since high school?"

How could she think that? "One night," he

said. "One night, when I was on leave and lonely."

She blew out a disgusted breath. "Why should I believe you?"

There was really no reason she should. He tried to explain why he hadn't been honest, because he didn't think she'd heard him the first time. "She felt that Zinnia would be harmed by the association with her. She wanted Zinnia to have a fresh start."

"A fresh start." She stared at him. "If you really wanted to keep the connection a secret, then why on earth did you bring her back to Holiday Point?"

He was questioning that himself. Why had he, again? "It was what Chelsea asked me to do. Plus, I wanted to be near my family, at least Cam. And my grandmother. I guess I thought that, maybe, there'd come a time when it was okay to reveal that—"

"You took her to my parents' house," she said, pacing back and forth, glaring at him and then looking away. "You took their granddaughter to their house and didn't tell them the connection. You knew they wanted grandkids. I told you that!"

"Kelly—" He broke off, aware that nothing he could say would fix what he'd done wrong.

She wasn't going to listen to his explanations, and why should she?

"I thought you cared for me," she said. "You told me you cared for me. You *kissed* me like you cared."

He stepped toward her, reached for her. "I *do* care, Kelly. So much. That's why I made a plan to talk to the pastor after the holidays—"

She looked up at the ceiling, arms spread wide. "You made a plan. I'll say you made a plan. It must have been complicated to figure out how to deceive all of us, but you were able to figure *that* plan out just fine." She pounded her fist in her open hand. "I am *so bad* at choosing men. Man, I thought Danny was a jerk."

He blew out a sigh. There was no way this discussion was going to fix what he'd done wrong. "What do you want to do?"

"I don't know!" she burst out. "How should I know what to do?"

"Maybe we should talk about it tomorrow."

She rolled her eyes. "I've had enough of your talk," she said. "Look, Zinnia is my…" Her voice broke.

He started to speak, but she raised a hand, stopping him. "Zinnia is my niece," she choked out. "I love her. But I want nothing to do with you."

Chapter Thirteen

All the makeup in the world couldn't conceal
the fact that Kelly had had a sleepless night
and a miserable morning. She knew it, and it
put her in an even worse mood as she pulled
into the church parking lot in her just-repaired
car, Pokey beside her. She hadn't had a moment of peace since she'd discovered the truth
about Zinnia.

She'd checked on the toddler, who seemed
to have made a speedy and complete recovery.
She'd avoided Alec and had stayed away from
this morning's services, but she'd dragged herself here out of a sense of obligation. Six or
seven people were talking and laughing as they
carried things into the church. Or maybe out of
it? Kelly suddenly couldn't remember the plan
for the day. Her brain felt terribly foggy.

"Hey, girl! Thought you were meeting us at

the nursing home." Olivia had emerged from the church building, a steaming food tray in hand. She handed it off to the team loading the van and then walked to where Kelly was standing beside her car. "I thought Alec was coming, too."

"No." The single word came out of a thick throat.

Kelly hadn't realized how much she'd come to care for Alec until she'd learned of his betrayal. The fact that he'd kept the identity of Zinnia's mom from her, from everyone in Holiday Point, filled her with alternating grief and rage and other emotions that were hard to name.

All night, her thoughts had raced in an endless circle.

She would think of what she'd learned and get furious. That would lead her to remembering the multiple times Alec could have told her the truth about Zinnia but hadn't. But thinking back was treacherous, because she'd remember the good things: his laugh, his friendly willingness to help, his loving care of Zinnia.

His kiss.

It had all been fake, but she hadn't known it. That was because she was terrible, absolutely terrible, at figuring out what a man was really like. She had zero judgment when it came to relationships, and she knew it. So why, within months of being hurt by Danny, had she gone and fallen for Alec?

Because she had, in fact, fallen for him. She couldn't deny it. He was so handsome, so apparently kind, so caring. And that smile…

She'd picture it and melt inside. And then her mind created other, more painful pictures. Alec sharing that smile with Chelsea. Having a relationship with Chelsea. Making a child with her.

There was so much she didn't know about the situation. When had they gotten together, and for how long? What had happened that had caused them to break apart? Did he know more than Kelly and her parents did about Chelsea's last days?

She ought to ask him, for her parents' sake, but she couldn't bear to look at him. That was why she'd rushed out of the house without checking the details of this afternoon's volunteer job.

"So," Olivia said, "want to talk about it?"

"About *what*?" Kelly snapped.

"About whatever happened that made you look like you're going to either melt down or murder someone."

Kelly squeezed her eyes shut for a moment and then looked at Olivia and shook her head. "I can't talk about it right now, but soon, okay?"

Pokey leaned against her leg and whined, clearly sensing her distress.

"Of course." Olivia looked at her with concern. "You're still coming to the nursing home today, aren't you?"

"I don't know." Kelly looked up at the sky, hoping to keep the ocean of tears inside her from flowing out. "I can't think."

At least, she couldn't think about practical things, like what to do in the moment. Instead, her mind circled Alec's giant, awful revelation, over and over again.

Olivia took Kelly's hand and tugged her toward her battered subcompact. "Come on. The group needs help delivering the food, and the residents need cheering up. They'll be disappointed if Pokey doesn't show."

"Okay, sure." She looked doubtfully into the car's tiny back seat. "You don't mind if Pokey rides in your car? We can take mine."

"Pokey can fit. And I think it's better if you don't drive."

Did she appear to be that badly off? Actually, maybe Olivia was right. She urged Pokey into the back of the car and then squeezed into the passenger seat.

Kelly knew from experience that when emotional disaster struck, it was important to keep moving. To continue your day-to-day routines, and to get out of yourself and your own misery by helping others.

She swallowed her feelings and scrolled to Eldora's number. She'd let her great-aunt know that they were going to an event at the nursing home that adjoined the senior apartments where Eldora lived. Maybe Eldora would like to come along.

Her aunt texted back right away. Not feeling well, staying close to home.

Are you okay? Need anything?

No, thanks, just taking it easy. Have fun.

Olivia chatted as they drove the twenty minutes to the place. She was clearly trying to distract Kelly from her troubles, and she didn't seem to mind that Kelly wasn't keeping up her side of the conversation.

Soon they arrived, pulling in right behind the van carrying the food. With Pokey on a leash, Kelly couldn't carry a big load, but she took a bag of bread and rolls from another visitor who was struggling.

Inside, a tall Christmas tree dominated the open area where the event was to take place. Wreaths were displayed at every window, and a gingerbread house and ceramic reindeer sat on a tabletop.

Someone had spent a lot of time decorating, and the place was cheerful. Kelly's spirits lifted, just a little.

No matter that her heart had just been broken, no matter how angry she was, she could still have her life. She had good friends like Olivia, who was so loyal and always had Kelly's back. She had her church, which was known for friendliness and community outreach. She and Pokey could help others.

It was a good life. She knew it, and she was sure she'd start to feel it again soon.

Pokey started straining at the leash, eager to get to the residents who were coming into the big room. Or...no. Just no.

Pokey was straining toward a corner of the room, where a conversational grouping of chairs was located.

Seated together were Alec, his grandmother and Zinnia.

Pokey was wagging her tail, eager to visit some of her favorite people. Zinnia hadn't spotted Pokey yet, though, so Kelly tugged the dog toward a group of people near the big Christmas tree. Pokey, always amenable to making new friends, trotted at Kelly's side and soon was greeting a man in a wheelchair, who'd sat slumped until he spotted the dog. Seeing Pokey, he reached out and petted her head, smiling. His touch was a little rough and uncoordinated, but Pokey handled it like the pro she was.

Kelly stood with the tree blocking her from the view of the corner group and tried to breathe deeply. Just the sight of Alec made her stomach clench and her heart hurt.

And Zinnia. Kelly hadn't seen the girl since Alec had dropped his bombshell, except for that quick check when the child was sleeping. But the glimpse she'd caught just now had nearly taken Kelly's breath away.

Zinnia was Chelsea's child.

Why hadn't Kelly analyzed her parents' statement that Zinnia looked so much like Chelsea had as a little girl, in her pageant pictures? A couple of people had even commented on the resemblance, she remembered now, when Zinnia had tried on her new Christmas dress.

And Alec had stood there, not saying anything, smug with his secret.

She needed to leave. She'd come to the senior apartments to feel better, and instead, she'd seen the very person who'd betrayed her. If she stayed, she'd have to interact with him in front of a crowd. She'd have to pretend that everything was just fine.

She looked around for Olivia. Her musical

friend sat at the piano, speaking with a couple of residents and another visitor from the church. Then Olivia nodded and started playing *"Good King Wenceslas."* One of her companions sang along, while the other nodded, and as Kelly watched, two more residents wheeled over to the piano to join in.

Kelly couldn't ask Olivia to leave. She couldn't pull her friend away from making the elders happy.

Kelly sucked in a breath and let it out in a sigh. Okay. She was here, and she was stuck here, and she needed to grow up and participate in the event.

If only she could avoid Alec and Zinnia, she might even survive it.

Alec couldn't believe Kelly was there. In fact, he wasn't 100 percent sure that he'd seen her at all.

But there was Pokey, and when he leaned back in his chair, he could see the edge of Kelly's sweater, the gold of her hair.

He'd come to pay a Christmas Eve visit to his grandmother. He'd visited her twice since they'd arrived, and she was great company and loved the visits. It was good for his grandmother *and* Zinnia to get to know each other. They were already bonding.

So this visit was a good thing all around. He'd thought it would be a relief for Kelly if he and Zinnia weren't underfoot while she processed what had happened. He'd wanted to stay out of her hair.

Instead, he'd come to the exact place where she was intending to spend the afternoon.

He couldn't believe the truth had come out that way. He should have hidden Zinnia's birth certificate, he supposed, so that he could have found a gentle way to reveal the truth.

But even the thought of hiding anything made him sick with guilt.

He'd hurt and enraged Kelly, and he hated that he'd done that. Throughout the sleepless night, every time he closed his eyes, her anguished face had appeared in his head.

One thing she'd said stuck out: Why did you even come back here?

He knew why he had. He wanted to provide a safe home for Zinnia, where she could grow up surrounded by good people and by the parts of his family that had it together enough to be positive influences. Wanted her to grow up with cousins. Wanted her to know her great-grandmother while there was still time. It was what Chelsea had wanted, too.

It wasn't only for Zinnia; it was for him, too. He'd always longed to be part of a community, and it had been looking like Holiday Point was going to be the place to do that.

He watched as Kelly emerged from behind the tree, glanced in their direction, and then turned her back and walked away. To make things easier for Kelly, he knew he should leave. He should make it so encounters like this wouldn't happen anymore. Indeed, he'd spent the morning calling around to see if there was another place they could stay, but all the hotel rooms and Airbnbs in the area were booked or closed for the holiday.

He stared morosely in the direction Kelly had gone. She stood now at the center of a group of three men, two white-haired and one completely bald. They were paying attention to Pokey, but mostly, they seemed to be flirting with Kelly.

And why not? She was beautiful and sweet and kind. Knowing her as well as he did, he could see that her smiles and laughs were a little forced, but she was trying. Because she was a good person.

Even in the midst of her pain and anger, she'd come here to help others. That was who she was.

"So what's wrong?" his grandmother asked. "How are things with your friend Kelly?"

He opened his mouth to say something innocuous, and found he couldn't stomach even that much deception. "I messed it up," he said. "I did something really wrong, and she's through with me."

"Did she say that?"

He nodded. He couldn't get her words out of his mind: *I want nothing to do with you.*

"Can it be fixed?"

He shook his head and decided to come clean with his grandmother. Now that Kelly knew, it was only a matter of time until her parents and then the rest of the town knew. "Keep this to yourself for now," he said, "but Zinnia's mom is Kelly's sister, Chelsea."

His grandmother stared. "The one you dated in high school?"

He looked down at Zinnia. She was playing with the set of multicultural dolls Gram had gotten her, totally preoccupied.

"Uh-huh. We got together briefly when I was on leave, and that's how Zinnia came to be." He kept his voice low.

"Oh, my." She shook her head slowly. "And you didn't want to tell Kelly and her family?"

"I wanted to, but Chelsea made me promise to keep the secret. She felt that her bad reputation in Holiday Point would keep Zinnia from being accepted."

"That's just plain silly," Gram said. "If there's any family that has a bad reputation, it's ours, and everyone knows about it. And they've treated Zinnia just fine despite our problems, haven't they?"

"Yes." As he thought back, he realized it was true. When they'd actually been in the presence of Fiscus acting up, a few people had looked askance at him, but for the most part, people understood. Whatever adults did, children weren't at fault.

"Here's what I think." Gram leaned closer, also keeping her voice low. "It's been good for you to be here in Holiday Point. Selfishly, of course, I've loved spending time with you and getting to know my great-granddaughter. But it's also good for Cam. It's been hard for him, being the only decent-acting person in the family. Having you here has put a spring in his step."

"It's great for me, too," Alec said. "And for Zinnia. I love that she has cousins here."

"Exactly." Gram's brow wrinkled. "I also think there's a chance it'll be good for your parents."

He started to disagree.

She held up a hand. "I know, they seem pretty far gone into the party life," she said. "But the only thing that's nudged them, or your mother at least, in the right direction, is the chance to get to know Cam's kids. Having Zinnia here is just going to add to the motivation to turn her life around."

He smiled a little and then blew out a breath. "You're piling on the guilt, you know."

"Don't feel guilty," she said instantly. "Just don't give up on us and on Holiday Point quite yet."

One of her friends came over then, with news to share, and Alec turned to let them talk and to check on Zinnia.

Only Zinnia wasn't there. He stood and scanned the room and saw her toddling determinedly toward Kelly and Pokey, who stood beside the refreshment table.

He might have let her go, only he saw Kelly's stricken face. Seeing Zinnia had to be hard for her. He hustled after his daughter.

"Pokey!" Zinnia exclaimed as she reached the dog and wrapped her arms around her.

He'd explained to her before that most dogs didn't like hugs, but maybe she sensed the tension in her father or in Kelly.

Zinnia squeezed tighter, and Alec increased the length of his strides. He reached her just as Kelly knelt down and spoke gently.

Of course, Kelly would never take her feelings out on a little girl. It wasn't in her to do that, even though Zinnia refused to release Pokey.

"Honey, you're hurting Pokey," he said as he knelt beside Zinnia and the dog. "Let go. Then you can do the two-finger touch."

"Hug," Zinnia said, her lower lip thrusting out. She squeezed Pokey tighter.

"Let go right now." He made his voice stern, and Zinnia, who hadn't heard that tone often from him, started to cry. She continued to cling to Pokey, although she did loosen her grip a little.

Pokey, thankfully, wasn't getting aggressive, but Alec knew from experience that Zinnia could be strong enough to hurt someone.

"I'm sorry," he said to Kelly, who stood above them, tension in every line of her face and body. He wanted to talk with her, to be with her, to laugh together about Zinnia's behavior and admire Pokey's gentle acceptance of the rough treatment. But that wasn't happening.

Gently, careful not to hurt either his daughter or the patient dog, he pried Zinnia's hands off Pokey.

Zinnia wailed and tried to reach for Pokey, but Alec kept her little hands firmly encased in his own.

Pokey backed off and made her way to Kelly's other side, watching Zinnia cautiously.

If he could get Zinnia settled, maybe he could talk to Kelly. But when he looked at her, he realized she was blinking back tears. And then she took Pokey's leash and rushed out of the room.

Everything in him longed to run after her. But

she didn't want him anywhere nearby. He carried the wailing Zinnia in the other direction, out into the lobby, waving off people's questions and offers to help.

He'd just seen how painful Zinnia's presence was for Kelly. That was a good argument in favor of taking Zinnia and moving away.

But his grandmother's words rung in his ears, too. Having him and Zinnia here was good for her, and for Cam, and maybe even for his parents.

And it was good for Zinnia, he knew that. It was good for him.

Zinnia's sobs were slowing down, and he sank into a chair and held her, rocking gently. Soon her crying turned into occasional gulps and plaintive repetitions of "Pokey, Pokey." She saw the dog every day, of course, would see her later tonight, but he knew reminding her of that wouldn't help. Toddlers weren't logical. He fumbled in his pocket, found a handkerchief, and wiped her tears.

Olivia strode into the lobby. "I need to talk to you," she said. She stood in front of him, hands on her hips. "What did you do to Kelly?"

Zinnia looked up at her, her expression fearful.

"Now's not the time," Alec said mildly, nodding at his daughter. "In fact, Zinnia and I are heading home for a nap. Would you mind letting my grandmother know?"

"I'll do that," Olivia said. "On one condition." She didn't move.

Alec eased around her, found Zinnia's coat on the rack, and helped her into it. "What's that?" he asked as he shrugged into his own coat.

"That you find a way to fix whatever you did," she said. "Kelly is a great person, and she doesn't deserve to be treated poorly. Not now, not ever."

She was right about that. "I'll try," he said without a lot of confidence, and Olivia glared at him and went back into the main room.

He carried his sleepy daughter out, confusion swirling as fast as the snowflakes that were starting to fall.

Fixing things with Kelly was unlikely to happen, not after what he'd done. In fact, the only way he could make things better for Kelly was to keep his distance from her.

His mind swirled with the question of where he and Zinnia should live. They weren't fully committed to being here in Holiday Point, not yet. Zinnia wasn't attached to a day care, and Alec hadn't found work or a place to live. Kelly's parents didn't yet know their connection to Zinnia, and maybe Kelly would keep that to herself if he and Zinnia left. The last thing he wanted to do was to cause pain to Kelly's parents.

It would be hard on Zinnia to make another change, but within six months, if they left, she'd have forgotten Gram and Cam and her cousins.

She'd have forgotten Kelly and Pokey.

Alec wouldn't forget. Not ever.

It was only now that he'd ruined all chances with Kelly that he realized how very much he cared.

He didn't want to be apart from her. In fact, he wanted to spend the rest of his life with her.

With impeccably bad timing, he'd managed to fall in love with the woman who had every reason to hate him.

Chapter Fourteen

Kelly hid out in the ladies' room until the sounds of the party died away. Then, she stepped cautiously out.

Olivia rushed over. "Where were you? Are you okay?"

"Hiding. Is he gone?"

"Alec? Yeah." Olivia nodded. "I gave him a piece of my mind. Come on, we've got to get this leftover food over to the homeless shelter before we go home, and it's bad out."

"Sure. Sorry." Kelly felt like she'd been run over by a bus. Her arms and legs felt weak, and all her initiative was gone. She was grateful to Olivia for taking control and telling her what to do.

As they walked out, Pokey alongside them, Olivia grabbed a box of tissues off an end table and thrust it into Kelly's hands. "Take this. Looks like you need it."

"We can't steal their tissues," Kelly protested, her voice shaky.

Olivia rolled her eyes. "I count four boxes in this room alone. I promise, I'll bring a case of tissues to donate the next time we visit. Now, come on, the car's loaded."

Kelly put on her coat and then knelt to put Pokey's sweater on. The greyhound licked her face, and she leaned her head against the dog for a second. Dogs were wonderful, simple and loyal. Unlike men.

Outside, the snow was coming down faster. They got into the little car and Olivia pulled out.

"Are you sure we shouldn't call someone for a ride?" Kelly asked as the car skidded a couple of feet to the side.

"We'll be okay. I'm good at snow driving." Indeed, Olivia handled the stick shift vehicle with skill, driving confidently but cautiously up and down the snowy hills toward the homeless shelter on the outskirts of Holiday Point.

"Can I do anything to help?" Kelly asked.

"Distract me. Tell me what's going on between you and Alec."

Kelly hesitated. But why not? Everyone in town would know soon. They'd know she was a dupe, fooled once again by a sweet-talking man. Not about romance, this time—at least, not that anyone knew—but about the identity of her niece.

She told the story, and Olivia hit the brakes and almost spun off the road. "Whoa. That's a distraction, for sure." She righted the car and proceeded forward. "He did that, really? Why?"

"Chelsea told him to," Kelly explained. "I guess—he felt more loyal to her than to anyone in this town, me included."

"Wow." Olivia glanced over at her. "Hurts, when you've gotten involved with him."

"I didn't get...okay. I did get involved. Or at least, I have feelings." Kelly used her mitten to rub condensation off the windshield. "He was in a relationship with Chelsea. I can never compare with her."

"Hold on." Olivia pulled into the parking lot of the shelter, a low brick building. She stopped the car and then turned to Kelly.

She was glaring. "Don't you *ever* say anything like that again. Get out of the Stone Age. Women shouldn't be comparing themselves to each other. We're all unique."

"Right, right, of course." Kelly pulled a tissue from the box on her lap and blew her nose.

"You're a beautiful woman, and you're loving and kind. Way more loving and kind than Chelsea, if you have to compare."

Kelly knew it was true. Something in Chelsea had prevented her from thinking of others. She'd lacked empathy and compassion. For the first time, Kelly imagined Chelsea as a mother, trying to care for a baby and put its needs first.

Could Chelsea have done that? Had she changed that much? She had a brief, sharp desire to ask Alec what Chelsea had been like as a mother.

She stifled it.

"Alec would be so blessed to have you as a partner, instead of her," Olivia went on. "And what's more, I think he knows it. Did he say his relationship with Chelsea was serious?"

Kelly thought back on their tearful, conflict-ridden conversation. "No," she said slowly. "He said it was for one night. When he was home on leave."

"Huh." Olivia frowned. "Obviously that's not ideal. But cut him a break. It's hard to fight for your country."

"It is," Kelly admitted. "And God worked it for good, making Zinnia."

"That's for sure. She's a dear child."

"But," Kelly said, "he lied to me. I fell for a bad guy again."

"Alec's not *bad*," Olivia said.

"He's a liar." Even saying the words hurt. "I want to be a strong single woman, and I'm not doing it. I barely have Danny in the rearview mirror, and here I am getting my heart broken again."

"When you open your heart, you get hurt." Olivia shrugged. "Believe me, I know that." Olivia didn't look at her as she said it.

Kelly studied her friend. She realized that there were big areas of Olivia's life she didn't share. "How do you know it?"

"This isn't about me, it's about you. Just… think about how hard it was for him. He was trying to make the best decision for Zinnia and to keep his promise to your sister. It was a no-win situation."

"He screwed up. Big time." But Olivia's words made her consider the possibility that Alec's actions could have been a tiny bit understandable.

"I know he cares for you. It's on his face, every time he looks at you."

Kelly wished that were true, but she didn't believe it. Olivia was just being kind. "We should take that food in and get home before the weather gets even worse."

"Yes, we should. Promise to think about all this, and to stop putting yourself down?"

"I'll try," Kelly said. And she would. Whether she'd succeed or not was anyone's guess.

Alec had stopped to see Cam and drop off gifts, and they'd talked briefly. Zinnia was tired,

though, and the snow was coming down hard.
Alec left quickly, with plans to see everyone the
next day if the roads were clear. Zinnia instantly
fell asleep in the car, which was good because
it allowed Alec to focus on his driving, but bad
because she might not sleep tonight.

The more he thought about it, the more he
realized he would have to leave Holiday Point.
He couldn't continue to cause Kelly that kind of
pain. He cared about her more than anyone else
in the world except Zinnia, and Zinnia would
thrive wherever she was.

They passed through town. Dusk was falling,
and it seemed like every home and shop in town
was lit up, multicolored lights and white ones,
inflatable Santas and tasteful nativities. Holiday Point took its responsibilities as a Christmas town seriously. So much fun for kids. For
everyone, really.

It would be hard to leave this warmhearted
place.

They were just a quarter mile out of town,
heading toward the river house, when someone
came into the roadway. It was a man, waving
his arms, and Alec braked hard and swerved to
avoid hitting him.

What an idiot.

He pulled as far to the side of the road as he

safely could and then squinted through the snow at the man approaching him. Oh.

Of course, it was Fiscus. No coat, no hat, no gloves. Furious at his brother for his apparent death wish, Alec lowered the window. "What are you *doing*?"

"Come on!" Fiscus was out of breath. "This way."

"You'd better get in. You'll freeze."

"No! Over here! There's a lady hurt. Do you have water?"

Alec always carried a water bottle, and he grabbed it and handed it to his brother. "I have Zinnia," he said, angling his head toward the back seat. "Where's this lady?"

"Pull up fifty yards and you'll be right behind her." He turned and strode into the snowy dimness.

Alec pulled up. His heart turned over when he recognized Eldora's car, its nose pointing down into a ditch.

He glanced back at Zinnia—amazingly, still sleeping—jumped out of the car, and hurried to Eldora's vehicle.

She was behind the wheel, leaning back against the headrest, face pale and eyes closed. Fiscus's coat was draped over her.

Adrenaline flooded him. "Was she conscious when you found her?"

"She's in and out. We need to make her drink something, if she wakes up, and get her to the ER regardless. She's dehydrated beyond what she can take in by drinking, and they'll be able to check the contusion on her forehead. Let's get her into your vehicle."

It was as if his younger brother was a different person: serious, sober and competent. The thing he rarely remembered about Fiscus flashed into Alec's mind: he'd been a medic in the army, a good one.

They cleared space for Eldora in Alec's vehicle, leaning the front seat back, and then carefully moved her there. Alec pulled an emergency road flare from the back of his vehicle and hastily set it up to warn other vehicles away from her damaged car. "Call the police while I drive," he told Fiscus. "I doubt they'll be able to get out here and tow her car tonight, but they should know it's here."

"Need to use your phone."

Alec hesitated just for a second, then handed it to him and told Fiscus the password. He was ashamed of the part of himself that didn't trust his brother. Even though there was reason for it, Alec didn't want to be that kind of person.

Eldora was trying to speak. "No…fuss," she said, and then lapsed back into unconsciousness.

Alec focused on the road. "Good Sam's still the best hospital to take her?"

"Yeah."

Alec headed in that direction, steering past the turnoff to the river house. Eldora hadn't gotten far before she'd wrecked her car. Whether it had happened as a result of the road conditions or whatever health issues she was having didn't matter for now. They just had to get her to the hospital.

Behind him, he heard Fiscus speaking to the police, and then to the hospital. Zinnia fussed a little, and Alec heard his brother's soothing murmur. He glanced in the mirror and saw that Zinnia's eyes were closing as Fiscus gently stroked her sweater-clad arm.

They reached a stretch of road that the highway department had cleared. "What were you doing out there without a vehicle?" he asked his brother.

"Taking a walk. Tell you later."

"Okay." It was a weird time and place for a walk, and of course, with Fiscus, Alec was unlikely to get the whole story. "Kelly Walsh is in my contacts. Can you call her and tell her what's happening?"

"No problem. You can tell me about *her* later."

The misery of the past two days with Kelly

washed over Alec, but he forced himself to focus on the task at hand. He drove carefully along the slick highway. Once, he spotted a deer's glowing eyes beside the road and braked, but the creature didn't leave the woods, and they passed safely by.

"Kelly's not answering," Fiscus said. "Anyone else?"

"I'd say Kelly's parents, but I don't have a number."

"No…fuss," Eldora said again. Her face, when he glanced over, seemed even paler. "Where…taking…me?"

Fiscus leaned forward and put a hand on Eldora's shoulder. "To the ER, but just for a bit, and then you can go home."

That seemed to be the right thing to say, because Eldora didn't protest. Minutes later, Alec saw the lights of the Good Samaritan hospital complex ahead. He searched out the ER and pulled in.

Fiscus handed him back his phone and got out to speak to the paramedics. They quickly helped Eldora out of the car and onto a gurney. "Meet you inside," Fiscus said, and walked alongside Eldora.

Alec was worried about Eldora, but the transformation in his brother was cause for hope. He parked and tried calling Kelly.

No answer; just a "this number is unavailable" message. Had she blocked him? He tried texting, but again, there was no response.

He stuck his phone in his pocket, collected Zinnia and her things, and headed into the hospital.

Chapter Fifteen

Kelly pulled the third sheet of cookies out of the oven, set them on the cooling tray, and slid the fourth sheet in.

It was Christmas Eve, and the cinnamon-and-vanilla smell of snickerdoodles filled the air. Normally, Kelly would have tasted about six of them; that was why she wore loose-fitting clothes when she was baking.

Now, though, she didn't have the appetite.

The house was eerily silent. She was grateful for Pokey, who lay sprawled on the kitchen floor, long legs to one side, watching Kelly's every move. It was a mark of the dog's loyalty that she was in here on the kitchen's tile floor rather than in front of the fire on such a cold night. She was intuitive and had probably sensed that Kelly needed company.

Kelly didn't have to be alone. After their

discussion and Kelly's meltdown outside the homeless shelter, Olivia had wanted Kelly to come spend the night at her tiny apartment. It would be fun, she'd said, and they could walk to Christmas Eve services together rather than driving more on the treacherous roads.

Although Kelly had appreciated the offer, she'd declined. She'd told Olivia she wanted to be with Eldora, but the truth was, Kelly wanted to lick her wounds without an audience. Plus, she didn't feel like she would be good company. She'd already inflicted enough of her emotional distress on her friend.

It turned out that Eldora wasn't home. Had she gone to church in this weather? Or maybe she was visiting a friend. She hadn't mentioned having Christmas Eve plans. But then again, Kelly hadn't exactly been warm and communicative with her great-aunt—with anyone—in the past twenty-four hours. She felt bad that she didn't know how Eldora had decided to spend the holiday.

She refused to descend into self-pity. "Being alone on Christmas Eve isn't the worst thing that could happen," she told Pokey firmly.

The greyhound lifted her head and studied Kelly with her big brown eyes.

"It's a part of being a strong single person,"

Kelly continued. "Sometimes you'll be alone on a holiday. And it's fine."

Pokey's ears drooped and she rested her head on her paws, watching Kelly.

"It *is* fine. I'll bake cookies for everyone I know. I'll bake all night."

Pokey let out a gusty sigh.

Outside, she could see in the floodlight that illuminated the driveway that the snow continued to fall, though not as heavily as before. Kelly put on Christmas music and started mixing up a batch of snowball cookie dough. She chopped pecans by hand rather than getting out the food processor, then creamed butter and sugar and vanilla together.

Keeping busy was supposed to keep thoughts of Alec away, but it didn't.

He'd tried to call several times, and a part of her desperately wanted to answer. To talk to him, find out where he and Zinnia were, hear what he had to say.

To forgive him.

But that was just weakness. She tended to be too eager for friendships and relationships to work out. Especially with Danny, she'd put up with too much and ignored the signs that the relationship was in trouble.

She wouldn't make that mistake again. The evidence that Alec didn't truly care for her was so big and obvious that even she couldn't miss it. She didn't want to listen to excuses and explanations. Didn't want to be persuaded by her own soft feelings.

She'd turned her phone off and put it away.

Alec had lied to her. He'd had a relationship with her sister, and Zinnia was the result.

She couldn't get around the pain of that.

He'd probably only acted loving with her because Chelsea was gone. In a small town during the holidays, he'd had to take what he could get, which was her. But what he really wanted was Chelsea, gorgeous Chelsea.

Yes, he'd said that it was just one night. But if he'd lied about everything else, maybe he'd lied about that, too.

She finished adding the pecans, flour and salt into the wet ingredients and put the bowl in the refrigerator to chill. Then she sat cross-legged on the floor beside Pokey.

The kitchen smelled wonderful, full of rich, buttery cookie fragrance. The Christmas music was upbeat and festive. Eldora had made a pretty display of evergreen branches and red candles and top-hatted snowmen on the windowsill over the sink, and she'd put up a Christmas valance.

None of it lifted Kelly's mood.

"Why do I keep choosing the wrong guy, Pokey? Why?"

Pokey didn't answer, of course; in fact, she started to snore.

Kelly closed her eyes and ran her hands along the dog's bony back. She really shouldn't be talking to her dog. She should be talking to God.

After a few minutes, she did. She started by thanking Him for her many blessings: a warm place to stay, a sweet dog, a loving family, good friends. A job where she could make a difference. A friendly, uplifting church family.

Thinking about her blessings made her feel better, as always, but the minute she stopped listing them, her pain rushed back in and she struggled with God.

What did He want from her? Why couldn't she have a nice husband and kids like so many people seemed to get so effortlessly?

Why had He let Chelsea go off the rails?

She wondered if Chelsea was with Him now, looking down. To her knowledge, Chelsea hadn't attended church after leaving Holiday Point. Still, church attendance wasn't a requirement for having faith.

For the first time, she thought about what it might have been like for Chelsea at the end. Had she known she was dying? Had she regretted leaving Zinnia behind?

A memory came to her then: Chelsea, putting her favorite battered doll to bed each night in a wooden cradle their dad had made. Mom had patched together a quilt, she remembered, and wrapped it in a package under the tree with the doll's name on it. Chelsea had been so thrilled. She'd rushed to find the baby doll and had wrapped it in the blanket and cuddled it close.

Kelly drew in a breath and let it out slowly. Zinnia was such a sweet, loving little girl. No matter what Chelsea's problems had been— and they'd been huge, leading to her death— she must have showered love on her baby. A neglected, unloved child was unlikely to have the sunny disposition Zinnia had.

All of a sudden, she was hungry to hear the story of Zinnia's early years. She wanted to know what her sister had been like as a mother.

She missed the big sister Chelsea had been during the early years of their childhood.

A montage of images passed through her mind now. Chelsea teaching her to ride a bike. Chelsea cutting the hair off all of their Barbie dolls and then sobbing with regret. Chelsea defending her against a bully in school.

Kelly had been too angry to think of the good things for years, but now, they came flooding back to her, and she cried for the loss: to her, to her parents, to Zinnia.

She had no idea why God had allowed Chelsea's potential to go to waste. It was one of those things their pastor talked about on a regular basis. They couldn't know God's plan, couldn't understand everything, not while they were on this earth.

She went into the living room and found her Bible. Pokey ambled in, stretching backward and forward, and then stood by the fireplace and looked at Kelly.

"You're spoiled, you know?" She turned on the fire and then sank into an armchair beside it, flipping through her Bible.

There it was, the passage in First Corinthians: *For now we see through a glass, darkly; but then face to face: now I know in part, but then shall I know even as also I am known.*

Did Chelsea see clearly now?

Would she, Kelly, come to understand why life was working out differently than what she'd wanted or planned?

She leaned her head back and closed her eyes. It wasn't the verse you'd normally associate with Christmas Eve, but God had known what she needed and put it into her head.

Thank You, she whispered. She still hurt, still felt terribly upset with Alec. But the complexity of the situation, and her inability to understand it fully by earthly means, had pushed away some of the pain.

Pokey sat up and gave a sharp bark, then trotted toward the back door. Kelly stood and followed, stopping for a quick check in the hall mirror to make sure she wasn't too red-eyed or mascara-messed. It must be Eldora, and Kelly didn't want to bring her down.

Or maybe it's Alec.

Kelly refused to analyze the leap of her heart at the thought.

There was a pounding at the door, and then the door opened. "Yoo-hoo, Kelly? It's Mom and Dad."

Okay, not what she'd expected. She hurried to help with the packages they were carrying while Pokey ran in circles around them. Cold air and snowflakes blew in through the open door, and Kelly was about to close it when another car pulled up. What in the world?

"We were worried about you when you didn't answer your phone," Mom said, "so we decided to come check on you. Actually, we brought our gifts over. Hoping we can spend the night here, rather than all by ourselves."

"Roads are bad," Dad commented, turning to squint at the other vehicle. "Now, who could that be?"

Kelly and her father peered out, and Kelly's heart turned over. It was Alec.

But not *just* Alec. His brother Fiscus climbed out of the back seat and opened the passenger door. He was helping someone out.

Eldora?

Moments later, Eldora was walking into the house, holding onto Fiscus's arm. Alec followed, carrying Zinnia.

Suddenly, Kelly wasn't alone at all.

In the chaos, she was able to sneak a few glances at Alec, and once, she caught him looking back at her. He didn't smile, and neither did she.

She refocused on Eldora, who was saying something about a hospital visit.

Kelly gasped. "What?"

"What happened?" Kelly's mom hurried to take Eldora's coat.

Eldora waved a dismissive hand. "I'm fine. Just a quick IV and I feel one hundred percent better."

"But why did you need an IV?"

Eldora rolled her eyes. "I was foolish. Felt queasy, so I didn't have anything to eat or drink, and that made me feel worse. So I thought it would be a great idea to drive myself to the hospital. I didn't count on the bad roads."

Fiscus took up the story. "Glad I was out at

the right moment to see her go off the road. Alec and I got her to the hospital, but we couldn't make her stay."

"She checked herself out," Alec said, his voice rueful. "Fiscus is a trained medic. Okay if he hangs out here tonight?"

"Cookies smell good," Dad said, eyeing the dozens cooling on the counter.

It wasn't what she'd expected of Christmas Eve, and she still ached every time she looked at Alec. She needed to be some kind of hostess, though. "Everyone come in, there's a warm fire," she said, "and I'll make hot chocolate and coffee." Suddenly, she felt so, so tired. "Then I think I'm going to go to bed."

By the time Alec got Zinnia settled in her bed, he was exhausted. He was demoralized, too. Being around Kelly, knowing that she hated him, was rough.

She was so pretty. Even in no makeup and an old sweatshirt and jeans, even though she looked like she'd been crying, she was everything he'd ever wanted in a woman.

Her being upset made him long to comfort her, but he knew he was the last person who could do that.

Kelly's parents had gotten Eldora settled and were sitting by the fire, drinking hot chocolate Kelly had prepared. Kelly was nowhere in sight.

Since he couldn't be with Kelly, he wanted oblivion. He wanted to go to bed and try to sleep.

But when he looked at Fiscus, he could tell that his brother was uncomfortable being around Kelly's family. He probably needed a drink, too, and he probably couldn't reach his AA sponsor, if he had one, on Christmas Eve.

He beckoned to his brother. "The snow is stopping," he said. "Let's find some shovels. We'll do the walkways, at least. Then we can get some sleep."

"Sure." Fiscus's voice was almost enthusiastic, so Alec knew he had been right. Fiscus needed something to do right now, a way to be useful. So did Alec, for that matter. They found some shovels in the basement of the river house and went outside.

Not only had the snow stopped, but moonlight shone through the clouds, making sparkly glitter on the snow. They start shoveling the long walkway that led to the front door.

For several moments, the only sound was the scraping of their shovels and the soft thud of the heavy snow they scooped up and tossed to the side. "So what's your plan going forward?" he asked Fiscus.

"I need AA," Fiscus said. "I know I do. It's just a question of making myself do it."

"What about that girl you were with last night, at Mom and Dad's?" Alec asked. "She sure seemed to like you." That was putting it mildly. The woman had been all over Fiscus.

Fiscus waved a hand. "Easy come, easy go. I'm not cut out for relationships."

Alec snorted. "Are any of us? We didn't exactly have good role models."

"That's for sure." They shoveled for a few minutes. This snow was dense and heavy, but to Alec, it felt good to work his muscles. Better than using his brain.

"You could do it," Fiscus said suddenly.

"Do what?"

"Have a relationship. With Kelly. I mean, look at Cam. He grew up like we did, and he managed it."

"That's Cam, and I'm happy for him." Alec shook his head. "But it's not for me. I wrecked it."

Kelly hated him because of his lies, or at least, his deception. Once her parents found out about it, they would hate him too. Hostility from some of the best people in town would not be good. He might have to leave.

He said as much to Fiscus, and his brother stopped shoveling. "You've got to be kidding me. You're going to let that go?" He gestured toward the house.

"Let what go?"

"All of it! That family. And a really good woman."

"Who hates me," Alec said.

"Why does she hate you? She's not a hater."

"Because I did something she can't forgive." And there in the moonlight, leaning on his shovel, he explained the truth to his brother. That Zinnia was Chelsea's child, and that he had concealed that reality from everyone in town.

Fiscus stared at him for a long moment, and then he started shoveling again. Alec did, too. There was nothing more to say.

The air around them was still. No wind. The moon came out more fully, creating shadows on the snow, and below them, on the river. Along the banks, ice formed lacy statues on the dried reeds.

Finally, Fiscus stopped shoveling and Alec saw that they had finished the walkway. "Chelsea, huh?" was all he said.

"One night. But I can't regret it, because of Zinnia."

"She's a gem," Fiscus said. "They both are. Zinnia, and Kelly, too."

They walked over to the driveway and started shoveling a pathway from the cars to the house.

"She doesn't want anything to do with me," Alec explained as they worked. "I concealed something huge, something that's incredibly important to her family. I don't blame her for wanting me out of her life."

Fiscus tossed a shovelful of snow to the side. It made sparkles in the moonlight as it fell. "You did it to keep a promise, right?"

"Right, but obviously, Kelly doesn't like it. The promise was to her sister."

"I know what else she probably doesn't like," Fiscus said. "Chelsea was a beauty queen and Kelly's just cute. People have said that in town ever since I can remember. She can't like being in competition with her sister, even her dead sister."

Kelly, just cute? Fiscus must not be seeing the same incredibly appealing woman Alec was. Alec puffed out a breath and waved his hand. "Sure, Chelsea was a classic beauty. But if you were around her for five minutes, you'd know better than to get involved." Alec used his foot to push the shovel into a patch of ice and break it up.

"So she wasn't the love of your life."

Alec shook his head. "One night. And back in high school, a few months. There was no depth to it. We didn't love each other, not really."

"Kelly was there, for the high school part at

least. Watching it happen. She needs to know how you feel. That it's different from what you felt for Chelsea, if it is."

"It's completely different." Alec stopped and stared at the icy ground as realization broke over him.

He loved Kelly. Loved her heart and her soul, loved her laughter and her tears, loved all of her. Unfortunately, he hadn't realized it in time to do the right thing. "It's over," he said.

"Over before it starts? That sounds like some stinkin' thinkin' to me."

Alec knew "stinkin' thinkin'" was a phrase from Alcoholics Anonymous, referring to the way alcoholics tended to justify their poor behavior, especially getting back into drinking. But could it refer to him, too? Was he wrong in how he was thinking about this? Fiscus was no dummy.

"You could have all this." Fiscus waved his arm toward the house.

Alec knew what his brother meant, because it was everything Alec wanted: a safe place and a community for himself and especially for Zinnia.

"You could live here and raise your daughter here, be a part of everything in the town. I can't. I've burned my bridges. But you could, maybe."

"So could you," Alec said. He meant it. The

last few hours he had spent with Fiscus had reminded him of what his brother was like when sober. He was a good man.

"This isn't about me." Fiscus pointed toward the house. "You have some talking to do. You have to tell that child's grandparents. If nothing else, Kelly needs them to know so she can have their help, figure out how to cope with it all."

Alec scooped the last shovelful of snow from the walk. Then he leaned on his shovel. He was wrung out. "Tomorrow," he said.

"Uh-uh." Fiscus shook his head. "If there's one thing I've learned, it's not to put things off until tomorrow."

"But—"

"Do it now, brother," Fiscus said. "I'll be here to pick up the pieces if they throw you out."

"You're probably right." Alec felt the strangest urge to hug his brother, but instead, he whacked him lightly on the shoulder. "Thanks," he said. Then he sucked in a breath and looked at the house. Could he really do this tonight?

There were still lights on inside. Somebody was still up.

"I'll finish this." Fiscus held out his hand for Alec's shovel. "You go on and do what you need to do."

"You're okay?" He meant with the urge for alcohol.

Fiscus seemed to understand. "I don't have anything to drink and I can't get anywhere to get anything, so yeah."

"Good. Okay." Alec started walking toward the house, his heart pounding. How would Kelly's parents react to the knowledge that they were Zinnia's grandparents?

Chapter Sixteen

"I have something to tell you." With those words, Alec was committed.

He felt like he had when entering into a dangerous sector overseas, though the cheery fireplace complete with Pokey sleeping in front of it, Kelly's smiling parents, the smell of hot chocolate and cookies, was the total opposite of a war zone. It looked like a Christmas movie in here.

Mr. and Mrs. Walsh smiled at him. "Come sit," Mrs. Walsh said. "I'll get you some hot chocolate."

Heaven forgive him, but he nodded, just because he needed a moment.

All too soon she was back, handing him a mug with a Christmas tree on the side and a peppermint-stick stirrer. "Here you go," she said. "Now, dear, what's going on?"

He sucked in a breath and opened his mouth.

There was a flopping, padding sound on the stairs, and they all looked in that direction. Pokey's tail thumped.

It was Kelly.

When she saw him sitting with her parents, she stopped.

"Come on down, honey," Mrs. Walsh said. "Alec wants to talk to us, and I'm sure it's okay if you're here, too. Isn't it?" she asked, turning toward Alec.

"Of course, if she wants to be here." He met Kelly's eyes. "She already knows."

Kelly came down, slowly. She was wearing plaid flannels and red fuzzy slippers, and Alec loved her so much it hurt.

But her expression, her frown, reminded him that it didn't matter. She'd already made her decision about him. What remained to him was to tell the truth to these good people in the hopes that it would at least do Zinnia some good.

He breathed in the evergreen smell from the boughs Eldora and Kelly had placed on the mantel. He cupped his hands around the warm mug. "You know I was involved with Chelsea in high school."

Both of Kelly's parents nodded, looking puzzled.

He cleared his throat. "Almost four years ago, I was stateside, on leave, and Chelsea and I got in touch. I had a stopover in Phoenix and we got together."

Mr. Walsh's brow creased. "Was she into the drugs then?" he asked sharply.

"I think she was."

Kelly made a rolling motion with her hand. Her message was clear: *get to the point.*

He sucked in a breath. "I *wasn't* into drugs, but I was drinking and partying too much. We spent a night together. And then I went back overseas."

Mr. Walsh's eyes narrowed, as if he were starting to guess where this was going. Mrs. Walsh looked puzzled.

Kelly's face was stone. Pokey stood, stretched, and went to lean against Kelly's leg.

"After that," he continued, "toward the end of my tour, I got myself together and made some changes. I came home and straightened out more, got work in California."

Mrs. Walsh frowned and nodded. Obviously she wondered why he was telling them about his past.

"And then Chelsea called." He paused, swallowed. "She'd had a baby. My baby."

Kelly's mother's eyes widened and she gasped, then let out a little cry. Mr. Walsh moved his chair closer and took her hand, and Kelly went to her other side. Pokey whined and sat down squarely on Mrs. Walsh's feet.

They were a unified family and Alec was on the outside. So be it; it was no more than he deserved. But he had to get it all out now, in the hopes that Zinnia could be a part of them.

"Chelsea wasn't doing too well," he continued. "She'd straightened out during her pregnancy, apparently, but she'd started using again. She felt she wasn't doing a good job as a mother, and she needed help."

They were all staring at him, various levels of understanding on each face.

"Of course I visited right away. Gave money to help her support..." He trailed off.

"Zinnia," Kelly's dad said. "It was Zinnia, wasn't it?"

Alec nodded.

Mrs. Walsh had tears rolling down her face. Outside, wind gusted, making the house shake. He and Fiscus would have to shovel again tomorrow.

If he were here tomorrow. If they hadn't thrown him out into the snow.

All he could do for them now was to finish the story. "I could see that Chelsea was having trouble." He broke off. Refocused. "As soon as I could, I found work in Phoenix and moved there."

Kelly's father cleared his throat. "Were you involved with her at that point?"

Alec shook his head. "Trying to co-parent, that's all. We never had a real relationship, I'm sorry to say."

Kelly crossed her arms over her chest.

"Anyway, I took over a lot of the parenting. Tried to encourage Chelsea to get into rehab, and she did, once, but it didn't take." His throat tightened. "You know what happened."

Kelly's mother leaned forward, buried her face in her hands, and sobbed. Her father's eyes were wet, too.

Kelly put her arms around her mother and glared at Alec.

Mr. Walsh spoke. "Were you there at the end?"

"No, sir, but close to it. When I saw she was going way downhill, I gathered Zinnia's things and took her home with me, then called 911."

"You were there near the end, though." It was the first thing Kelly had said to him.

He blew out a breath. "I was. The last time I saw her, she was pretty well out of it. I did what I could, but it wasn't enough." He hesitated. "I did pray with her, several times during her last months. Talked to her about how faith could change her life. The last time I picked Zinnia up, there was a Bible out on the coffee table."

They were all silent for a few minutes.

"You think she died a believer?" Kelly's mother asked.

Alec nodded. "I do."

"What happened next, after she passed?" Kelly's father asked.

"I needed to stay in Phoenix a little while, on the job. I needed to put as much money aside for Zinnia as I could. She had a good babysitter who helped her deal with the...the loss."

"We came to Phoenix when...when she died," Kelly said. "The hospital contacted us. Didn't it occur to you that we would? And that we might like to know about Zinnia?"

"Chelsea made me promise to keep her identity a secret," he said. "From you, and from everyone here in Holiday Point. She...well, she had realized the error of her ways. She wanted me to bring Zinnia back here, but she thought that if people knew she was Zinnia's mom, it would hurt Zinnia's chance to fit in and be accepted."

Kelly's eyes were wide, and she lifted her hands, palms up. "And you *listened* to her? Didn't you know us at all? Didn't you know this town?"

Alec looked at the floor between his feet. "I felt like I had to keep my word. It was all I could give her, and...keeping my word is important to me."

Kelly started to speak.

He held up a hand. "I know. I know now that I

was wrong and that keeping all of this to myself hurt people. Hurt you." He looked from one face to the next. "I take responsibility and I apologize. From the bottom of my heart. Although I know that will never make things right."

There. He'd said it all. He bowed his head and for the first time this evening, he prayed. For the people he'd hurt, and for Zinnia.

"Alec." Kelly's mom's wavering voice made him look up.

She held out her arms.

Alec felt like saying, "Me?"

"Come here and let me hug you. You're Chelsea's baby's father."

He made his way forward, his own eyes blurry, and clasped the woman in his arms. She hugged him back, hard.

When they parted, his first thought was for Kelly. Would her mom's warmth enrage her further?

Kelly's mother looked at her husband. "We have a grandchild. Zinnia is our grandchild." She stood. "I have to go look at her. Oh, my word, I love her so much already." She reached out and hugged Alec again. "Thank you for all you've done for her. Thank you for being a good father."

"I'm sorry," he said through a thick throat.

"You're forgiven. All I ask is that you let us be a part of her life."

"Of course."

Kelly's mom had forgiven him instantly, but she wasn't the only one in the room. Alec looked at Kelly's father.

The man nodded, stepped forward, and put an arm around Alec. "You've done well with her. Now we want to help."

Their generosity of spirit stunned Alec. He'd never experienced anything like it.

He looked over in Kelly's direction.

But she wasn't there. Sometime in the swirl of emotions, she must have slipped out.

That made things clear. Her parents' forgiving spirit didn't extend to Kelly. And he didn't blame her at all. He didn't deserve forgiveness.

The moment Kelly saw her mother on Christmas morning, the question burst out of her. "How could you forgive him so easily?"

Her mother glanced at her and then set down the carton of eggs she'd just pulled from the refrigerator. She came over and folded Kelly into a hug. "Merry Christmas, honey."

"Merry Christmas, Mom." She hugged her mother back and then stepped away. "I'm so glad you're here. But how—"

"Help me out here," her mother interrupted, picking up the egg carton and putting it into Kelly's hands. "Break eight eggs and beat them."

Numbly, Kelly did as her mother ordered. Then Pokey ambled in, and Kelly took the dog outside to do her business. The day was bright, sunshine sparkling on snow. Her breath, and Pokey's, made clouds in the cold air.

She felt numb after a restless night. She'd tossed and turned as Alec's story had churned in her mind. It was all so wild, so much.

Back inside, Mom had poured coffee for both of them. "Sit down a minute," she said.

Kelly sat and sipped coffee.

Mom was lining a pan with dough, the crust of her annual Christmas breakfast casserole. She looked over at Kelly. "That sweet child is part of our family. We *have* to love her. I already do."

"I do, too," Kelly said. "She's an awesome kid anyway, but to learn that she's Chelsea's daughter…" Her throat tightened annoyingly, and she coughed and then took a big gulp of coffee. "It's Alec I can't forgive."

"He made a big mistake, and he hurt you."

"He hurt you, too!"

Mom was grating cheese. "Of course, I wish I'd known of Zinnia from the moment she was born, but that's really on Chelsea, isn't it? A lot of this is on Chelsea." Mom abandoned her task and walked over to the paper towel rack. She grabbed a towel and wiped her eyes. "Zinnia looked so much like Chelsea that day in her fancy dress. I'm surprised we didn't guess earlier."

Kelly sipped coffee while her mother got her composure back, then went to the refrigerator. "Want me to make the fruit salad?"

"Yes. That would be wonderful," her mom replied.

So Kelly started pulling grapefruit and oranges out of the fridge. They'd all need to be peeled, which would take time. And hopefully, give her a focus other than her anger.

Mom blew her nose and washed her hands and went back to grating cheese. "As to how to forgive, well…seventy times seven, right? Isn't that what Jesus told Peter in the Bible?"

"Yes, but—" Kelly shook her head. "I just don't feel like it's possible. I don't see how you can be so nice about it all."

"Honey, I have so much to be forgiven for. I've made so many mistakes. How can I condemn the man who's been doing his best to raise our grandchild on his own?" She came over and hugged Kelly from behind.

Pokey must have sensed their distraction. She put her paws on the counter and started scarfing down grated cheese.

"Pokey, no!" Kelly and her mother cried out at the same time. They both rushed over, and

Pokey backed away, licking her chops. Kelly scolded her while her mother discarded all of the dog-tainted cheese.

Kelly's mom reluctantly agreed to substitute a bag of pre-shredded cheese that Kelly had on hand, and Kelly banished Pokey to the fireplace room under her dad's supervision. Then both of them got serious about their breakfast-preparation efforts. It wouldn't be long before Eldora and Alec and Zinnia converged on the Christmas tree and, family drama or not, everyone would eventually want breakfast.

"Don't let Alec's mistakes ruin your chance to see what could happen with him," her Mom said as she poured the egg mixture into the crust she'd prepared.

"What do you mean?"

"I've seen how you look at each other."

Kelly moved a heap of orange and grapefruit peels into the trash. "Mom, he was with *Chelsea*," she said. "I can't get past that. How could he even look at me?"

"And that's my number one sin," her mom said. "We should never have put Chelsea into pageants or let people make so much of her looks. It hurt her and it hurt you, though you came through it so much better."

You didn't put me into pageants because I wasn't pretty enough. But her mom was right in the sense that being gorgeous hadn't done Chelsea any good.

"I'm so proud of you, honey," her mom continued as she wiped the counter, "but in this area, thinking you're less attractive than Chelsea, you've sold yourself short. You've dated any man who asked you out, when you should have been so much more discriminating."

Kelly blinked. "You think I've gone out with anyone who asked me?" Was it true?

"I'm sure not just anyone, but you've said 'yes' when you should have waited for something better." Mom plunked her rolling pin into a sinkful of soapy water. "Why, that Danny, I could... I could hit him with this rolling pin!" She whisked it out and swung it threateningly, sending droplets of water everywhere. "Getting engaged to that awful Tonya in front of everyone!"

Laughter bubbled up inside of Kelly. "I'm glad you're on my side," she said. "Danny and Tonya deserve each other."

"They do," Mom said. "They surely do."

The sound of a high-pitched squeal came from upstairs, and despite her complicated feelings, Kelly was glad she could share Christmas morning with a little child. Her niece.

She wasn't just Kelly anymore, she was Aunt Kelly. She tried on the title and found she liked it.

Her mom checked the casserole in the oven

and then came over to pat Kelly on the back. "We're all sinners, and Jesus came into the world on Christmas to save us all. Remember that. And don't let your hurt feelings or your fears keep you from the happiness you deserve."

Kelly turned and hugged her mother. "Merry Christmas, Mom. And thank you."

"I love you, honey. Now, hurry up and finish that fruit salad. I'm going to go see my grand-daughter." Her voice was shaky on the last word. Having a granddaughter was, of course, mixed with grief and loss for her mom. But she was embracing the joy of it anyway.

Kelly definitely had a lot to learn from her mother and a lot to think about, this Christmas morning.

When had Alec ever had a Christmas morning like this one?

Of course, Zinnia was central. He'd never had her on Christmas before. Last year, he'd taken her to the children's service on Christmas Eve, but then he'd had to return her to Chelsea, who understandably had wanted to be with her daughter on Christmas morning. At that point, he'd had misgivings about Chelsea's ability to take good care of Zinnia, but she'd seemed sober, or close to it, when he'd dropped Zinnia off. He'd turned down an invitation from a church friend to Christmas dinner, and had instead watched TV and eaten take-out Chinese food. Just as he'd done most holidays as an adult, at least when he wasn't on base.

As for their childhood Christmases…they hadn't been awful, but they'd been nothing like this.

Eldora sat on the couch, dressed in jeans and a Christmas sweatshirt and looking perfectly healthy. Fiscus was beside her, and he appeared more rested and healthy than usual, too. Several days without drinking would do that for a man.

Pokey wandered around, tail wagging, flopping down occasionally to play with her new squeaky toy.

Kelly's parents sat on the floor with Zinnia, helping her rip into a gift they'd brought. Of course, when they'd bought it, they wouldn't have known Zinnia was their grandchild. And Alec knew money wasn't plentiful for them. Still, they'd bought her a big stuffed animal, just because she was a child in their life. Zinnia hugged it and rolled around on the floor with it, cute as a button in her footed pajamas.

He couldn't believe how open Kelly's parents were to him, offering grace he didn't deserve. They'd hugged him as soon as he'd come downstairs, and they included him in their conversation. What was more important, they seemed ready to jump in and be Zinnia's grandparents. They couldn't stop hugging her and taking pictures of her.

Zinnia was little enough that she didn't really understand what it was all about. She was as excited by the wrappings as by the gifts. Especially since both Kelly and her mom had chosen pink wrapping paper and bows.

Kelly. He watched as she opened gifts and thanked people with a reasonable approximation of serenity. After her anger about learning the secret of Zinnia's parentage, he'd come downstairs today not sure whether he and Zinnia would be able to be in the same room with her or not, let alone participate in family rituals.

But she'd been fine. Not super welcoming like her parents, but she'd greeted him in a way that was at least neutral, and she'd hugged Zinnia.

The gift opening went on for a while, with lots of smiles and laughter. They'd even come up with a couple of gifts for Fiscus. Eldora had passed him a wrapped box containing a flannel shirt that must have been intended for Alec or for Kelly's dad. What a kind woman. Fiscus had tried it on as soon as he'd gotten it open, over his T-shirt, and he'd thanked Eldora profusely. Kelly had wrapped up a box of cookies for Fiscus, and when he opened those, he'd eaten a couple right away and raved about them before passing the box around. He was fitting in better than Alec would have ever expected.

When Alec handed his gift to Kelly, she'd finally had to look at him. She'd bitten her lip and then taken it and opened it. It was a book of Christian poetry, and she thanked him and flipped through it. Then she'd whispered to Zinnia, and Zinnia had taken a present from under the tree and brought it to Alec.

It was the latest military thriller by one of his favorite authors, in hardback. She must have noticed that he'd gone through the first couple of books in the series, used paperback versions, during the time they'd stayed together at the river house.

It wasn't an extravagant holiday. Most gifts were small and inexpensive. But the group felt warm and loving and fun. Once the gift part was over, Kelly and her mother disappeared to the kitchen, and soon everyone was invited to the table. Kelly's father said a prayer, and then they all dug into breakfast casserole and fruit salad and buttery rolls.

Fiscus caught his eye and gave a thumbs-up. In the gesture, Alec saw mirrored his own appreciation of the family gathering.

No one brought up last night's revelations. There would be time to talk about them, but not today. Today was for celebrating.

He appreciated that this loving family had taken him and Fiscus and Zinnia in. Appreciated that Kelly wasn't refusing to be in the room with him.

But it wasn't enough.

Alec hadn't slept last night, not much, but he'd done a lot of thinking. He knew how he felt about Kelly.

And, since she wasn't completely closed off to him, he knew what to do. So after the breakfast dishes were done, he checked with Eldora and Fiscus and Kelly's mom to make sure they were fine with watching over Zinnia, and then he approached Kelly.

She was sitting by the Christmas tree, petting Pokey. Her hair shone in the sunlight that streamed through the window. Without a bit of makeup on her face, she looked fresh and sweet and beautiful.

"Would you like to go for a walk?" he asked her. And then he held his breath.

He knew the answer would likely be no, but he had to ask. Had to try for the thing he wanted, even if the chances of getting it were small.

She looked at him for a long moment "Uh... okay, I guess," she said finally, her voice wary. "Pokey could use a walk."

Alec had to restrain himself from pumping

his arm victoriously. The battle wasn't won, not by a long shot, but it wasn't over, either. He hadn't lost, not yet.

He helped her into her coat, and she put a Christmas sweater on Pokey—a little ridiculous, but he'd seen how the short-haired, skinny dog shivered and he knew a coat was a necessity— and they walked outside into the snowy air.

Now or never, he told himself, and sent up a silent prayer for divine assistance.

Kelly walked beside Alec, with Pokey trotting along on her other side. By unspoken agreement, they headed across the river toward town.

The world was quiet. Yesterday's storm had blanketed everything with a six-inch topping of heavy snow. The river flowed along, but ice coated the shallow areas along the bank and stiffened the reeds and grasses with a sparkling, frosty coating. Cold air chilled Kelly's cheeks and froze the air she breathed.

She didn't know how to feel. Her beliefs about Alec, Zinnia, her sister and life in general had undergone such shifts in the past two days that she felt numb, more numb than her toes in her furry boots.

Alec had lied. Or, if not exactly that—since she couldn't think of a time when he'd said something untrue about Zinnia's mother—he'd lied by omission big time, creating a deception for her family so complete it took her breath away.

Yet, her parents had forgiven him almost instantly.

He'd been upfront and sincere last night when he'd told them the truth. And she could kind of see why Chelsea had insisted on the secret. She *had* burned bridges here, and people tended to remember things like what she'd done. She was notorious in the town.

Kelly was almost certain people wouldn't take their anger at Chelsea out on an innocent child, but Chelsea had always been a little bit paranoid. She was also incredibly persuasive. It wasn't a stretch to think she'd decided Zinnia would be unsafe here if it was known she was Chelsea's daughter, and then talked Alec into believing it.

"Kelly, I asked you to come out walking for a reason," Alec said abruptly. "First off, I want to apologize."

"You did that last night."

"But I want to apologize to you specifically. I deceived you most of all, let you think Zinnia's mom was a stranger. That was cowardly of me. I'm embarrassed that I acted that way, and I'm sorry."

Kelly nodded. Their pace had slowed, but they were still moving forward.

"I… The thing is, I cared what you thought of me. I didn't want you to know about my lifestyle, or that I'd reconnected with your sister in a superficial way. I'm not that person anymore, but I need to own up to who I was."

"Having that lifestyle isn't any worse than deceiving people," she said quietly.

"That's true. What I did was wrong and hurtful, and I'm truly sorry."

They continued their slow stroll. The sun was almost blinding in its brightness. Kelly thought about what she'd discussed with her mother this morning. Thought of earlier talks with Olivia and with Eldora.

Did she want to be the kind of person who held grudges? "I accept your apology," she said, taking his arm. "I want us to stay friends. It's important to Zinnia. And to me, too."

"Thank you." He put a gloved hand over hers. "That means a lot."

They walked on, reaching the end of the bridge and entering town. No cars were out on the streets. A couple of kids were having a snowball fight, and a little girl rode what was obviously a new bike up and down the shoveled section of her driveway while her parents watched from the porch, arm in arm.

Alec steered Kelly away from the residential street and into the park. The giant Christmas tree was there, and a sleigh, and a couple of inflatable snowmen. When they walked by the large nativity scene, they could see that Baby Jesus was now in the manger.

"There's more I want to talk to you about, Kelly," Alec said.

Her heart gave an extra thump. "More secrets?"

"No. Never again." The sincerity in his eyes and tone convinced her he was telling the truth.

"Let's sit down over here." He guided her to a wooden bench in front of a picnic shelter. The brick wall behind the bench caught the sunshine and protected them from wind, making it almost warm. Indeed, Pokey turned around three times and then plopped down on the sunny pavement.

So much had happened in this park throughout her life. Most recently, she thought of watching Zinnia admire the Christmas trees, and the dog parade, and seeing Danny's proposal to Tonya.

She felt like she'd been knocked around by the events of the past few months, knocked into a place where she could no longer pretend she knew what was going to happen next or how she'd respond to it. All she could do was to utter a short prayer and then remember to rest in the Lord, who would work it all for good.

He put his arm along the back of the bench. "Sit down a minute," he said.

She did, and now that her anger had dissipated, now that she'd accepted his apology, she could enjoy the light touch of his arm on her shoulders.

"Kelly," he said, "I want you to know how I feel about you."

She opened her mouth. It was in her mind to say "You don't have to do that," but she suddenly realized she was selling herself short, thinking he was only being nice.

Just listen, God seemed to say.

"I've always liked you," he said. "Always thought you were a great person."

Wonderful. Just how every woman wanted to be perceived: as a great person.

A blue jay hopped from a pine branch to a picnic table, scolding.

Just listen.

Alec went on. "Since we've been spending all this time together, it's become so much more. You're good and kind, always trying to help other people. You're hard working, and I admire that. You've embraced Zinnia, even without knowing your blood connection to her, and your caring attitude has made a world of difference to her."

"Thanks," she said. She was trying to listen without judgment, but this "you're a good human being" speech sounded an awful lot like the one Danny had given her as a lead-in to breaking up.

Just listen.

"I'm trying to reassure you that my feelings have a basis in everyday, practical reality, but Kelly…" He took off his glove and touched her hair, almost reverently. "You are just so appealing to me. So beautiful."

That was a tough one, and she started to protest and then pressed her lips together. Olivia always told her she was beautiful, and Mom said the same thing. Beauty was a complex thing. Maybe, even though she didn't have as big a dose of it as Chelsea, she had some of it.

She met his eyes and smiled. "Thank you. That's good to hear."

His arm tightened around her shoulders. "Can I be blunt?"

A shiver ran down her spine. "Um, I guess?"

"There's all kinds of pretty, and some kinds are more attractive to me—as a man—than others. Your hair, your style, your attitude, the way you move… I can't keep my eyes off you."

Heat suffused her cheeks and she had to look away, in part to hide the smile that wouldn't stay off her face.

Alec was still talking. "That kiss was the best

thing I've felt, ever, and I want like anything to do it again."

She focused her eyes on Pokey, because she felt like she might fly right off the bench and into the stratosphere if she didn't somehow keep herself grounded. "That's…a possibility," she managed to say.

A gust of wind swept around the building, cooling her warm face. She breathed slowly, trying to remain calm.

Alec's words were turning her world upside down. He felt *that* for her? Really?

He leaned over and brushed a light kiss across her lips. The heat from it traveled instantly from her head to her toes.

She reached for him, but he took her gloved hand, kissed it, and tucked it into his own. "I want more than a few kisses, Kelly. I've seen a lot of loss and I know that life is short. I want to…to court you."

Her eyes widened at the old-fashioned terminology. Could he mean what she thought he meant?

He squeezed her hand and then let it go, shaking his head. "I know my family isn't great. And I know I have a lot to make up for with the way I deceived you. I would never ask you to answer me today, or even soon, but know this—I love you, and I want to marry you."

It was as if all her bones turned to jelly. She could only stare at him.

He waited a few seconds as if to gauge her reaction, but she had no breath to speak.

"If there's no way, if you know for sure you could never see me that way, tell me and I'll back off. I hope we can always be friends, but if there's even the slightest possibility of more… let me try, Kelly. Let me try to win your heart."

He touched the side of his forefinger to her chin and she felt the slightest tremble.

This big, strong man, this father, this veteran, was shaking as he asked her to let him into her life.

He meant it. He loved her. He wanted to marry her.

The reality of God's plan swept over her, physically warming her the way the Bible reading she'd done last night had warmed her. God was in charge. He worked everything for good.

She wasn't as beautiful as her sister; she knew it. But the way he was looking at her, she believed she had the kind of beauty that mattered to him.

And she believed that, after what he'd said, he wouldn't end things on a whim like Danny had.

She could trust him. And she could trust her own feelings of…what? Love?

Yes, love. She was well on her way to falling in love with Alec.

Her fears took hold of her for a moment. *Calm down, don't get excited, don't expect too much.*

But then her mother's words from this morning came back to her. *Don't let your hurt feelings or your fears keep you from the happiness you deserve.*

Did she deserve happiness? Was this real? Or should she wait, hold off, learn to keep her heart closed even in the face of having a whole lot of loving feelings, more loving feelings than ever before in her life?

She sat back and looked up at the sky, limitless and blue. It was Christmas, and she was here with a man she cared for deeply. An imperfect man, but a good one. And he'd just told her he wanted to marry her.

Her dream of a husband to spend her life with, a family to cherish, could come true.

She looked upward for another moment, making sure. And then she took Alec's hands in hers and shared her heart. Shared all that she saw in him: that he was a hard worker, a family man, a good father. That he was kind, and fun to be with.

That he was as handsome as a movie star.

"I'm sorry I was so upset before," she said. "I'm not as quick to forgive as I should be, as my mom and dad are."

He pulled her close to his side. "You have no

reason to apologize. It's me who needs to make up for the mistakes I've made." He looked at her. "Really, you think you might come to care for me? Despite my mistakes? Despite my family?"

"No family is perfect, and no person is either. And yes, I could come to care for you. More than that, to love you."

She pressed a kiss to his cheek, and then he pulled her even closer, and they got a little lost in each other. But not for long. Pokey barked and nudged them with her nose until they laughed and stood and headed back to the river house.

Halfway there, church bells started to chime, and it occurred to Kelly: of course, this had happened at Christmas, the birthday of Jesus. Jesus had come to help people overcome their pasts and have new life.

And she had that now. Everything she'd ever dreamed of. The future had never looked so bright.

Epilogue

It was a gorgeous day in May when they said
their vows.

The doors of the church were propped open,
letting spring air into the foyer of the church
where Kelly stood with Olivia and Stacey, her best
teacher friend who was her other attendant. Dad
was kneeling down keeping Zinnia entertained,
and Pokey had flopped onto the floor to take a
nap, oblivious to the fancy lace kerchief around
her neck and the band around her thin torso.

Alec had given Kelly a beautiful ring on Val-
entine's Day, and they'd decided they didn't
want a long engagement. They couldn't wait to
live together as husband and wife. The months
since then had been a flurry of teaching her
first graders and doing therapy work with Pokey
and getting closer with Zinnia, who was doing
amazingly well. All from her good old garage

apartment. She'd forced her parents to accept rent for it, and she'd found them a tenant for when she moved out.

She loved them dearly, but it would be wonderful to have a home of her own, with Alec and Zinnia.

Alec had found a good job that he liked, and he'd rented a house down the street from her parents. They'd live there together once they were married, and her parents were delighted to spend lots of time with all of them, but especially Zinnia.

Kelly peeked into the sanctuary to get a glimpse of Alec, who waited at the front of the church while the music played. Fiscus and Cam stood beside him.

"They're a good-looking family," Olivia said.

"Stunning," agreed Stacey.

A loud argument on the steps of the church pulled their attention away from the handsome Wilkins men.

"Come on! I'm not going to this wedding by myself!"

"I'm coming, I'm *coming*!"

Olivia's jaw dropped and she turned to Kelly. "You did *not* invite Tonya to your wedding," she said.

"I invited the whole congregation," Kelly said. "I didn't think she'd come, though, or bring Danny along."

Kelly had heard that Tonya was pushing Danny to get married sooner rather than later, and that he was hedging about it. Whatever happened, she hoped it was for the best. She couldn't wish anyone anything but happiness on this happiest of days.

The music swelled and Stacey headed down the aisle as Tonya came into the church, pulling Danny by the hand. She looked Kelly up and down, her mouth twisting into a sneer. "Third time's a charm, huh?" she said.

"How dare you!" Olivia stepped forward, lifting her bouquet as if she were going to bring it down on Tonya's head.

"It's fine," Kelly said, grabbing her friend's arm and gesturing toward the church. "Go on. It's your turn."

Olivia glared at Tonya for a few more seconds and then started down the aisle, fulfilling her role as the maid of honor. Tonya and Danny slipped into the back row.

Kelly's dad stood, holding Zinnia's hand. "Almost time for you to do your thing, sweetie," he said to his beloved granddaughter.

Zinnia peeked into the church, and her eyes widened. There was definitely a crowd. It seemed like everyone in Holiday Point was here.

She took a step back. "Don't want to do it," she said, her lower lip trembling. "Scared."

Kelly knelt beside the frightened child. "Just walk to Daddy really slowly, like we practiced last night. Pokey will be right beside you. And remember, you get to scatter rose petals all the way." She handed Zinnia her flower-girl basket, then snapped her fingers for Pokey to come alongside her. She straightened the pillow affixed to Pokey's back, where the rings were tied securely with rose-colored ribbons.

"Okay," Zinnia said, her voice doubtful.

Kelly kissed her. "Now. Go!"

Zinnia hesitated, and Alec came out into the middle of the aisle and knelt down, beckoning to her.

Zinnia started running toward him, Pokey galloping beside her. Halfway there, Zinnia must have remembered her flower-scattering duties, because she stopped, reached into her basket, and grabbed a big handful of rose petals. She wound up like a major league pitcher and flung them at the people in the pews. Then she abandoned her basket and ran to Alec amid laughter from the attendees.

Pokey followed at a more sedate pace. When she got to the front of the church, she flopped down as if she needed a nap.

More laughter.

Eldora stepped in, unfastening the wedding rings from the carrier on Pokey's back and handing them to Cam. Kelly's mother guided Zinnia to her place in the front row.

The music changed, and the familiar chords of the wedding march started. Kelly's dad put an arm around her and then pointed to a tree just outside the church, covered with pink blooms.

In its branches, a cardinal trilled and chirped, its song audible even over the swelling organ music.

She met her father's eyes, shiny with unshed tears. Her own throat felt thick.

At their house, for years, a decorative plate had hung above the kitchen window. It depicted a cardinal in the center, with the symbolic meaning stenciled around the rim: *those we have lost will live forever, as long as we keep their memories alive in our hearts.*

Alec had shared more with Kelly and her parents about how, on a few sober occasions in her last weeks, Chelsea had offered up sincere prayers, asking for forgiveness and inviting Christ into her heart.

"If she sees, she's happy for you, as happy as that bird's song," Dad said gruffly. He pulled out a handkerchief and blew his nose.

Of course, this would be bittersweet for him. He'd had two daughters, but there remained only one to walk down the aisle.

Kelly hugged him, and they clung to each

other for a few seconds. "Come on," he said, loosening their embrace and crooking his elbow for her to hold. "Let's get you married."

Kelly kissed him on the cheek and then took his arm, and they walked forward. Through blurry eyes, Kelly saw so many dear friends. And at the front of the church was the man she loved more than anyone else in this world.

She felt like running toward him as Zinnia had. She was so very ready to start their life together. But she maintained her sedate pace. There was time. Plenty of time.

This was forever.

* * * * *

If you enjoyed this K-9 Companions book, be sure to look for Her Christmas Healing *by Mindy Obenhaus, available in December 2023, wherever Love Inspired books are sold!*

And look for these other K-9 Companions books also by Lee Tobin McClain:

Her Easter Prayer
The Veteran's Holiday Home
A Friend to Trust

Dear Reader:

Have you ever had to make a choice that didn't seem to have a right answer? We even have a phrase for it: the lesser of two evils. That's what happens to Alec in A Companion for Christmas. He wants the best for his daughter, but that seems to mean he can't tell the truth to Kelly, even though he's coming to care for her more deeply than he ever thought possible.

Because there's no good answer, Alec ends up hurting Kelly badly. He wonders if he can ever be forgiven. And then Kelly's parents offer a shining example of Christian grace, forgiving Alec instantly. It takes Kelly a little longer, but she ends up giving him grace, too. As a result, she's able to open up to the happiness and joy she never thought she'd find in this life.

We all make mistakes, and we all need forgiveness. Even Pokey commits a small sin when she steals the cheese off the counter on Christmas day! How fortunate we are to have a God who sees our sins, large and small, and showers forgiveness on us.

From my family to yours, I wish you a wonderful Christmas!

Warmest regards,
Lee

Get 3 FREE REWARDS!

We'll send you 2 FREE Books plus a FREE Mystery Gift.

Both the **Love Inspired®** and **Love Inspired® Suspense** series feature compelling novels filled with inspirational romance, faith, forgiveness and hope.

YES! Please send me 2 FREE novels from the Love Inspired or Love Inspired Suspense series and my FREE gift (gift is worth about $10 retail). After receiving them, if I don't wish to receive any more books, I can return the shipping statement marked "cancel." If I don't cancel, I will receive 6 brand-new Love Inspired Larger-Print books or Love Inspired Suspense Larger-Print books every month and be billed just $6.49 each in the U.S. or $6.74 each in Canada. That is a savings of at least 16% off the cover price. It's quite a bargain! Shipping and handling is just 50¢ per book in the U.S. and $1.25 per book in Canada.* I understand that accepting the 2 free books and gift places me under no obligation to buy anything. I can always return a shipment and cancel at any time by calling the number below. The free books and gift are mine to keep no matter what I decide.

Choose one:
☐ **Love Inspired Larger-Print**
(122/322 BPA GRPA)

☐ **Love Inspired Suspense Larger-Print**
(107/307 BPA GRPA)

☐ **Or Try Both!**
(122/322 & 107/307 BPA GRRP)

Name (please print)

Address   Apt. #

City   State/Province   Zip/Postal Code

Email: Please check this box ☐ if you would like to receive newsletters and promotional emails from Harlequin Enterprises ULC and its affiliates. You can unsubscribe anytime.

Mail to the Harlequin Reader Service:
IN U.S.A.: P.O. Box 1341, Buffalo, NY 14240-8531
IN CANADA: P.O. Box 603, Fort Erie, Ontario L2A 5X3

Want to try 2 free books from another series! Call 1-800-873-8635 or visit www.ReaderService.com.

*Terms and prices subject to change without notice. Prices do not include sales taxes, which will be charged (if applicable) based on your state or country of residence. Canadian residents will be charged applicable taxes. Offer not valid in Quebec. This offer is limited to one order per household. Books received may not be as shown. Not valid for current subscribers to the Love Inspired or Love Inspired Suspense series. All orders subject to approval. Credit or debit balances in a customer's account(s) may be offset by any other outstanding balance owed by or to the customer. Please allow 4 to 6 weeks for delivery. Offer available while quantities last.

LIRLIS23

Get 3 FREE REWARDS!

We'll send you 2 FREE Books plus a FREE Mystery Gift.

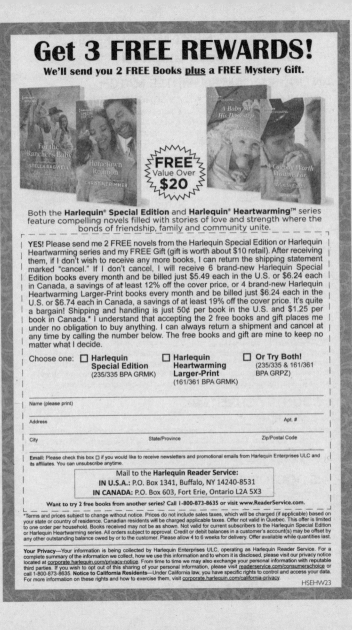

FREE
Value Over
$20

Both the **Harlequin® Special Edition** and **Harlequin® Heartwarming™** series feature compelling novels filled with stories of love and strength where the bonds of friendship, family and community unite.

YES! Please send me 2 FREE novels from the Harlequin Special Edition or Harlequin Heartwarming series and my FREE Gift (gift is worth about $10 retail). After receiving them, if I don't wish to receive any more books, I can return the shipping statement marked "cancel." If I don't cancel, I will receive 6 brand-new Harlequin Special Edition books every month and be billed just $5.49 each in the U.S. or $6.24 each in Canada, a savings of at least 12% off the cover price, or 4 brand-new Harlequin Heartwarming Larger-Print books every month and be billed just $6.24 each in the U.S. or $6.74 each in Canada, a savings of at least 19% off the cover price. It's quite a bargain! Shipping and handling is just 50¢ per book in the U.S. and $1.25 per book in Canada.* I understand that accepting the 2 free books and gift places me under no obligation to buy anything. I can always return a shipment and cancel at any time by calling the number below. The free books and gift are mine to keep no matter what I decide.

Choose one: ☐ **Harlequin**
Special Edition
(235/335 BPA GRMK)

☐ **Harlequin**
Heartwarming
Larger-Print
(161/361 BPA GRMK)

☐ **Or Try Both!**
(235/335 & 161/361
BPA GRPZ)

Name (please print)

Address   Apt. #

City   State/Province   Zip/Postal Code

Email: Please check this box ☐ if you would like to receive newsletters and promotional emails from Harlequin Enterprises ULC and its affiliates. You can unsubscribe anytime.

Mail to the Harlequin Reader Service:
IN U.S.A.: P.O. Box 1341, Buffalo, NY 14240-8531
IN CANADA: P.O. Box 603, Fort Erie, Ontario L2A 5X3

Want to try 2 free books from another series! Call 1-800-873-8635 or visit www.ReaderService.com.

*Terms and prices subject to change without notice. Prices do not include sales taxes, which will be charged (if applicable) based on your state or country of residence. Canadian residents will be charged applicable taxes. Offer not valid in Quebec. This offer is limited to one order per household. Books received may not be as shown. Not valid for current subscribers to the Harlequin Special Edition or Harlequin Heartwarming series. All orders subject to approval. Credit or debit balances in a customer's account(s) may be offset by any other outstanding balance owed by or to the customer. Please allow 4 to 6 weeks for delivery. Offer available while quantities last.

Your Privacy—Your information is being collected by Harlequin Enterprises ULC, operating as Harlequin Reader Service. For a complete summary of the information we collect, how we use this information and to whom it is disclosed, please visit our privacy notice located at corporate.harlequin.com/privacy-notice. From time to time we may also exchange your personal information with reputable third parties. If you wish to opt out of this sharing of your personal information, please visit readerservice.com/consumerchoice or call 1-800-873-8635. **Notice to California Residents**—Under California law, you have specific rights to control and access your data. For more information on these rights and how to exercise them, visit corporate.harlequin.com/california-privacy.

HSEHW23

COMING NEXT MONTH FROM
Love Inspired

AN UNUSUAL AMISH WINTER MATCH
Indiana Amish Market • by Vannetta Chapman

With his crops failing, Amish bachelor Ethan King already has enough problems.
He certainly doesn't need flighty Ada Yoder adding to his troubles. But when
a family emergency requires them to work together, they'll discover that the
biggest problem isn't their differences—it's their feelings for each other.

BONDING OVER THE AMISH BABY
by Pamela Desmond Wright

After a car accident, Dr. Caleb Sutter is stranded in a Texas Amish community.
Then he suddenly becomes the temporary guardian to a newborn, along with
pretty Amish teacher Rebecca Schroder. But the baby soon raises questions
about his family history, leading Caleb to a crossroads between his past—and a
future love...

THE COWBOY'S CHRISTMAS COMPROMISE
Wyoming Legacies • by Jill Kemerer

Recently divorced Dalton Cambridge can't afford to turn down a ranch manager
position—even if the boss is his ex-wife's new husband's ex-wife. Besides,
working for Erica Black is strictly business. But when he finds himself caring for
the single mother, will he risk everything for a holiday family?

THEIR HOLIDAY SECRET
by Betsy St. Amant

Preston Green will do anything for a fake girlfriend—even bid on one at
a charity auction. Lulu Boyd is the perfect choice to stop his mother's
matchmaking. And it's just for one holiday family dinner. Soon it feels all too
real...but another secret might make this their last Christmas together.

A COUNTRY CHRISTMAS
by Lisa Carter

Kelsey Summerfield is thrilled to plan her grandfather's upcoming wedding. But
the bride's grandson, Clay McKendry, is determined to keep the city girl's ideas
in check. When a series of disasters threaten to derail the big day, will they put
aside their differences...and find their own happily-ever-after?

THE DOCTOR'S CHRISTMAS DILEMMA
by Danielle Thorne

Once upon a time, Ben Cooper left town to become a big-city doctor. Now he's
back to run his father's clinic and spend Christmas with his daughter. Not to fall
for old love McKenzie Price. But when McKenzie helps Ben reconnect with his
little girl, will Ben accept this second chance at love?

**LOOK FOR THESE AND OTHER LOVE INSPIRED BOOKS WHEREVER
BOOKS ARE SOLD, INCLUDING MOST BOOKSTORES, SUPERMARKETS,
DISCOUNT STORES AND DRUGSTORES.**

LICNM0923

HARLEQUIN
PLUS

Try the best multimedia subscription service for romance readers like you!

Read, Watch and Play.

Experience the easiest way to get the romance content you crave.

Start your **FREE TRIAL** at
www.harlequinplus.com/freetrial.